MADDIE MAKES MONEY

SONIA GARRETT

Maria Montessori said:
"Respect all the reasonable
forms of activity in which
the child engages and try
to understand them."

Happy reading!

Sonia Garrett

What people are saying about
MADDIE MAKES A MOVIE...

———

For Jacquie,
Chase your dreams.

_____

THE LONGEST AND BEST EVER

"Put your hands on the slide, like this, and push off the ground," I say, showing Ben and Sam Granger my new parkour move.

Ben and I have been inseparable since our success in the Young Filmmaker of the Year Awards. He may only be in grade four, but he's pretty cool. Unfortunately, where Ben is, his younger brother Sam usually follows.

I grab the red plastic edges of the slide and kick off. The cold dew seeps through my fingerless gloves as I cartwheel over the playground equipment. My heart beats faster as the weight of my legs move over my body pulling me toward the ground.

Straighten your legs, I think to myself, seeing the basketball court upside down through the bright green taffeta skirt I'm wearing over my striped leggings.

Land it! Land it! I shout in my head, as one foot hits

the wet wood chips, wobbles, and I fall onto my knees. It's only my hands stopping me from falling flat on my face. *Still time to recover!* I throw my hands into the air, toss my head back, let my long curly hair fly off my face and shout, "Parkour!"

"Cool!" Ben and Sam shout.

"Cool?" Raquel Roberts, archenemy number one, laughs from the platform at the top of the climbing wall. Her groupies, Sunshine and Raine Finkle, copy the mocking snicker.

"I'll show you 'cool,'" Raquel says.

We all look up. There's a picture of One Direction staring down at me. "How come you're at school so early?" Raquel asks.

"It's a free country, isn't it?" I reply.

"Not when you break as many rules as you do. My mom says I have to stay away from you, Madeleine Moore. You're a 'bad influence' and need to be watched like a baby."

My blood boils. I stand up and place my hands on my hips. Then Ben slams into my knees as he tries to land his leap over the slide. We both tumble to the ground.

"Ha! Ha! Ha!" Raquel mocks. "You should stick to your skateboard, Wonder Girl."

"She can't ride it when she comes to school with us," Ben explains.

"Oh! Poor little mad Mads! Can't be trusted to get here alone," Raquel says.

"It's only on the days her mom works," Ben says.

I give him an evil look. I don't want Raquel knowing about my life. She always turns it against me.

"Your mom's working?" Raquel asks.

"What's wrong with that?" I reply. "Everyone's moms work, and mines always done some subbing. It's no biggy."

"My mom went back to work, and the next thing I knew Dad was moving out," Raquel says.

"My dad is not moving out!" I say.

"Well, if that's what you want to believe," Raquel sneers. "Parents keep the truth from us kids. My mom says film marriages don't last. It's only a matter of time before you'll be like me."

"I will NEVER be like you!"

"Wanna bet?"

"Just ignore her," my BFF, Leila Choudhury, says. "My parents are way more likely to split than yours, and they have nothing to do with making films."

"What?" I whisper. "What do you mean?"

"I overheard them last night," Leila says. "Dad says there's nothing for him in this country. He's going back to India."

"Your dad's always traveling, isn't he?"

"This is different. Mom had red eyes this morning, like she'd been crying. She said she had allergies, but she yanked my hair when she brushed it. She only does that when she's mad. Then Dad gave me a really long hug, and told me my report was the only thing worth coming home for."

My head tells me I should stay with my friend, but my feet shift from side to side looking for a way out.

"Watch me, Maddie," Sam shouts.

My head turns from Leila to Sam. He's donkey kicking over the slide. *Life's so easy when you're little. Sam plays, eats and pesters Ben and me. Leila is smiling but her eyes look really sad.*

"Leila, your dad won't move to India. You live here," I say.

"I think we'll move with him."

"What! You can't! You're my BFF."

"Come on, Maddie," Ben calls. "What's next?"

I wish I could split myself into two, so I can be with my friend, and still run around.

"Go on," Leila whispers. "I'll be okay. Just don't tell anyone."

"Are you sure?"

"Sure."

Leila and I do our funky hand jive: double fist bump, explosive jazz hands, clap right hands, then left, pat our bums and rub noses.

"Okay, now jump and grab the spider web," I say. "Swing your feet off the ground, land, throw your arms in the air and strike a pose. Parkour!"

"Parkour!" Ben and Sam shout.

Leila's sitting on the bench, watching us and smiling. I mouth the words, "Are you okay?" She nods her head.

Other children stand around and stare. *I love having an audience.*

"Leap across the pyramid using as few steps as possible," I say.

"Great jumps, Maddie! They'll be perfect for the Best Ever Regional Science Competition entry!" Ivan Vladivenski says, running towards me, holding a Ziploc bag out in front of his face.

Ivan's in my class. He thinks he's the best at everything, the best hockey player, the best looking and the best all round cool dude.

"I'm going to compare human jumping distances to animals. My dad's going to build me my own science lab when I win. Come on," Ivan says.

"What! No fair!" Ben says.

If I had my own lab, I'd make copies of myself, so part of me could sit with Leila, a clone would do parkour, and a third 'me' would see what this Science Competition is all about.

I look around. My audience is moving away. *I stopped for two seconds, and now, only Leila's watching me.*

Ivan runs to the soccer field, closely followed by Ben and Sam. He draws a line in the dirt with the heel of his new runners. Then he empties a pencil, notebook and an enormous metal measuring tape from the Ziplock bag. A computer printout falls out and flaps across the field. *If you can't beat'em, join'em.* I run after it and bend to pick it up. A gust of wind blows it away, again. I sprint after it and leap when the paper comes to a halt. Squelch! Muddy water splatters onto my smiley face socks and seeps into my runners. *Yuck! My socks look like poo emojis!*

I bend down, pick up the crumpled, soggy article and start reading it as I wander back to the group.

Jumping animal	Distance
Grasshopper	150cm (5 feet)
Frogs	180cm (6 feet)
Mountain Goats	3.5 metres (11.5 feet) long but known to jump off 50m (164 feet) cliff
Kangaroos	9m (29.5 feet)
Fleas	One hundred times their body length, that's the same as a human jumping 90m (295 feet)
Human world record	8.95m (29.3 feet)

Sam's standing on Ivan's line. He swings his arms, and jumps as far as he can. Ivan looks at the tape measure and says, "Fifty-two centimetres. Come on that's not even as far as a grasshopper."

"Ivan, I have an idea! I saw a group of acrobats at the circus doing amazing jumps. I'll show you!"

I run to the equipment area and step onto the yellow seat of the teeter-totter. "Ben and Ivan, stand up there," I say, pointing to the zip line platform. "When I count to three, you're both going to jump onto the other seat, and send me flying through the air. I bet I can jump as far as..." I pause, looking at the crumpled sheet in my hand. "A kangaroo!"

Ivan and Ben shrug their shoulders. They give each other a look. I turn my back to them so I can see where I'm going and count, "One, two, three!"

I can feel the boys landing at the other end.

"Lift off!" I shout.

Wow, I'm flying. I'm going even further than...

Bang! I land with my legs hitting the climbing wall; my body on the hard, metal platform; my hand, holding the soggy piece of paper, sliding over a pink cashmere sweater; and my face squashed into a picture of One Direction.

"Argh!" Raquel squeals. "Look what you've done to my new sweater!"

"Maddie!" Sunshine and Raine shout together.

"I'm telling!" Raquel says.

"If you wipe the mud off straight away, it may be okay," Leila says.

"If she's ruined this, she'll have to pay for it."

"We'll help you clean it," Sunshine says.

"Yeah, our mom's always wiping mud off us," Raine adds.

Their voices fade as the twins put their arms around Raquel and steer her away from the main school entrance, toward the door nearest the washrooms.

We may not have much time before Raquel tells on me, again. I look up and see the swings. *I have an idea!*

"Are you okay, Maddie?" Leila says.

I nod in reply, mentally checking I'm still in one piece and allowing my thoughts to take shape.

"That was cool!" Ivan shouts. "Three metres, forty-five centimetres. Wow, that's further than a frog!"

"Ivan, your project'll be way more exciting if it's about the inventions humans use to beat animal jumping distance. Y'know, like ski jumps, and human cannonballs. Oh, I know how I could do a bigger jump!" I say. "Some-times, when my dad gets blown up in a movie, he uses a Russian Swing. That way he gets lots of time in the air to throw his arms around, and make the movie look cool."

Raquel's comments about the film industry start

fizzing in my brain, but I pop the thought bubbles as they emerge. *My dad's job is awesome! He's a great stuntman, but he's not Brad Pitt or Tom Cruise. He's not about to leave us. I'll show Raquel. And I'm going to be just like him.*

"When the director calls 'Action!' Dad jumps from the swing and flies through the air. Come on! Let's try it!"

"Maddie," Leila whines. "Are you sure? Remember when you broke your arm, jumping off a swing."

"Stop worrying," I say. "That was in grade one, this is grade five. I'm ten and a half. What could go wrong?

"Ben, stand on the swing with me. Ivan, you get the measuring tape ready. I'm going to beat a kangaroo this time. How far do I need to jump?" I ask.

"Nine metres!" Ivan shouts. "That'd take you to here."

Ivan draws a line on the soccer field. Children stop their games and move toward the landing zone. An audience's gathering.

"Come on Ben," I say.

The swing gets higher and higher. The crowd gets bigger and bigger. My stomach feels as if it flips over at the highest point. *Oh boy. I have to do it. Just look at all those faces.*

I swallow hard. "Ben, I'm going to jump on the count of three. One." The swing travels forward. I look out over a sea of faces, close my eyes and take a deep breath. "Two." Ben and I fly backward with the ground passing below us really quickly. "THHHRRRREEEEEEEE!"

I let go and fly into the air.

"Madeleine Moore!" The deep voice of our principal, Mr. Richardson echoes across the playground.

I turn my head to see where he is, and my body follows.

Mr. Richardson is striding past the playground equipment with Raquel, Sunshine and Raine taking tiny running steps behind him.

No! Turn back! You have to spot your landing! I yell in my head, throwing my arms and legs in all directions.

Thud! My arms and back hit a wall of bodies. I tumble onto the stony field with other children falling like dominoes beside me.

I close my eyes, wishing an alien would abduct me, or a giant earthworm would appear and drag me into an underground tunnel.

"Ahhhh!" a child screams from under me.

I jump up. There's a small child lying on the ground. I recognize her from my 'buddy' class.

"Are you okay?" I ask.

The girl nods through her tears.

"Madeleine, take her to the office," Mr. Richardson says. "Mrs. McIntyre can check the damage you've done this time. Then we'll have a little chat about what you can, and can't do, on school property."

I take the girl's hand and start the long walk towards the school office where I know Mrs. McIntyre, our school administrator, will give me one of her 'looks' over the rim of her glasses. *Why do so many school days have to start like this?*

I glance over my shoulder. Mr. Richardson's watching my progress across the basketball court. His face is as set as the building I am heading to. *Do they teach 'Evil Looks' at Principal School?* Behind him, Ivan, Ben and Sam are stretching out the measuring tape and jumping about with excitement.

I pick up my pace, pulling the little girl just a bit faster. "Come on," I say. "Let's get this over with. I want to know whether I jumped further than a kangaroo."

2

WANNA BET?

School hallways always seem weird when they're empty; they echo and have a funny smell, like erasers, pine and barf. I wander back to my classroom with slow, heavy footsteps. The image of another Incident Report being added to my file weighs on my mind. If Mr. Richardson hadn't called my name when I was flying through the air, if Raquel hadn't gone to the office to tell on me, again, if Ivan hadn't gotten me involved with his silly Science Fair, I would've been the parkour coach until the bell rang and, now, I'd be in class like everyone else.

Life's so unfair when you're ten and a half. It was so easy when I was little.

I look at the collage snowmen on the wall outside my old kindergarten room.

Mr. Richardson's voice comes over the PA. "Good morning everyone. I apologize for the interruption. It has come to my attention that there've been some unsafe practices taking place on the swings. In order to prevent the closing of this piece of equipment ALL CHILDREN must follow these guidelines: Number one – Only one child may be on a swing at any time. Number two – The swing must be stationary when you get on and off it. There will be no more jumping off a moving swing. It simply isn't safe.

"Have a productive morning. And together, we'll make sure that everyone in our community learns, plays and grows, safely."

Oh, I could scream! I know what's safe and what's not. And distracting someone in the middle of a stunt's not safe. Now my class'll be halfway through their math sheet and I'll have to finish mine as homework.

My eyes start to sting. I'll get the blame for these new rules. *No tears. Not now. I can't let my enemy know she's got to me.* I hold the handle and swing open the door. *Empty! Where the heck are they?* I look around. There hasn't been a fire alarm. They're not under their desks pretending there's an earthquake. They're not hiding out of sight in case I'm a vicious intruder. *They're gone.* I panic. *What day is it? Tuesday. What do we have on Tuesday? Isn't it usually Math?*

School planners are out on the desks. There're a few water bottles, some pencil cases, and a collection of model tanks, lined up on George's desk. But grade five aren't here. I run to the library. Mrs. Austen, the librarian, is holding a picture book. A wave of little faces turn and stare at me. *Nope, not Library. Music?* I take off, running down the hallway.

Slow down. Use walking feet. My body won't listen to my brain. I slide down the stair railings and land just outside the Music Room. "London's Burning" is being screeched on recorders. *That's grade three.*

Where's my class? Are they outside playing Man Hunt without me? No, only a sub'd do that in the morning. That's it! We've got a sub who told them to get ready for announcements then peeled open her human disguise to reveal an alien, just as a space ship sucked everyone out of the window.

"Madeleine Moore, why are you still out of your classroom?" Mr. Richardson calls.

I can hear his polished shoes clicking on the vinyl floor.

"They're not there," I reply. "I've looked in the library. They're not in music. I'm looking for them, but they've disappeared. You should call the police! They're missing! The whole class has..."

"Try the gym," Mr. Richardson says. "I think you've a visitor, teaching the class drama. Not that you need any lessons on being dramatic."

I spin around, and walk as fast as I can back towards the stairs. I can hear the clip clop of Mr. Richardson's shoes behind me. *He's following me! Does he think I'll get lost?*

Standing outside the school gym, I take a breath and push the door open.

Everyone's eyes turn towards me. My class's standing in a circle watching Raquel's drama teacher, the guy from Dominic Drummond Drama who won all those prizes at the Young Filmmakers' Awards. My enemy's standing beside him with Sunshine and Raine glued to each other's side, right next to her. Raquel smirks at me.

"Maddie, I'm glad to see you found the note I left on the board. Come and join the circle. Mr. Drummond was just starting a warm up," Mr. Phillips, my real teacher, explains.

"Call me Dom, Dom the Dude," Dominic says,

striking a weird pop star stance. "Have you all made your gum nice and soft? Move your jaw and chew it well. Repeat after me. Sticky, sticky bubblegum."

"Sticky, sticky bubblegum," my class choruses.

I slide into the circle next to Leila, who gives me an 'are you okay?' look. I nod, and watch as she chews self-consciously on nothing.

"Now, take the gum out of your mouth," Dom says. "Oh no! It's stuck on your fingers. Try to shake it off. It won't budge. Swing your arm up high, down low, out to the side, all around you. And say, 'Sticky, sticky bubble gum.'"

"Ow!" Morgan yells as Ivan clips him on the side of his head.

"Be aware of your personal space," Dom says, in an airy voice, moving his hands around his large, soft stomach.

"Try taking the gum in your other hand. Oh hee haw! Now it's stuck there. Shake it off."

Everyone's copying our visiting drama teacher.

"Now, carefully try to scrape it off with your foot. Oh, you've just gone and gotten it stuck there. Shake your foot. It's not coming off. Try to scratch it off with the other foot. Now it's on that foot. Kick your leg in the air. Harder. Harder."

Karate and soccer kicks are filling the space around me.

"You jumped seven metres," Ivan whispers, using his

kicks to move closer to me. "I'll have to find a way to film you later as evidence for my project. Do you know that mountain goats can jump off fifty metre cliffs?

"I bet I could beat that," I say. "That's it! I have an idea!"

Leila nudges me in the side. I look up. Mr. Phillips is shaking his head and pointing towards 'Dom the Dude.'

"Later," I whisper to Ivan.

"One last enormous kick of your leg. Look, the gum has flown off into the air. Catch it in your mouth," Dom says.

"Errrr! Gross!" the class groans then laughs as one.

"Sit, hee-haw, sit, hee-haw, sit," Dom brays through a fake donkey-like laugh. "Oh, we can have so much fun together. Now, I'll need two volunteers to demonstrate our next game, 'Masters and Servants.'"

Hands shoot up around me. I don't feel like it, but I guess I should be brave enough to volunteer. After all, I want to perform stunts when I grow up. This has to be easier than getting set on fire. Slowly, I put my hand in the air.

"Let's have you, Raquel, and the wild leprechaun over there," Dom says.

The whole class bursts out laughing. I can feel my face burning as I look down at my green skirt and wild curly hair.

"That's Maddie," Mr. Phillips says.

"Of course, the winner of the first Movie Action prize

at the Young Film Awards," Dom says. "I'll have to put some stunts into my next film, and steal that one from you next year."

Dom laughs, but I can tell he meant what he said.

"Now, Raquel knows this game, so come, sit here, and be the master," Dominic says, bringing a chair near to the circle.

He rests his hands on my shoulders and pushes me next to Raquel.

"You are the servant. Your master can give you any order, and you have to mime, that means doing the action without props or speaking, whatever your master asks you to do."

This is not going to end well.

"Get me a drink!" Raquel orders.

I turn my back on Raquel, reach for a pretend glass, mime filling it up, and hand it to her.

"The more unreasonable the master is the more interesting the scene becomes," Dominic says. "See what happens if you don't like the drink."

"I don't want this! Where's the ice?" Raquel orders.

I put some ice cubes in the make-believe cup and roll my eyes. The whole class giggles as I hand the cup back to Raquel.

Dominic whispers into Raquel's ear.

"You've spilt some!" Raquel shouts. "Clean up this mess!"

"Oh! You're a natural, Raquel," Dom says. "You're born to rule the world."

I kneel down and act as if I am mopping up the spill with a cloth. The class is falling about laughing. More whispering from Dom. *Just wait until we switch parts and I get to order you about, Raquel Roberts.*

"Now, my shoes! Clean my shoes!" Raquel orders.

I look up in disbelief, only to see Dom pointing to his tongue.

"With your tongue!"

"What!" I shout.

My voice is drowned out by the shrieks of laughter coming from my class.

"And freeze!" Dom the Dude says. "Now, everyone find a partner."

Come on! Don't I get a chance to order Raquel around? You can't leave me on the floor like this!

There's a scurry of activity as everyone finds a partner to work with. Leila moves next to me.

"You're so good at this," Leila says. "I would have died if he chose me."

"Label yourselves A and B," Dom says. "As are the masters first."

I look around the gym while Leila is making me a Scoobie Snack with chicken, salad, peanut butter, honey, banana, Oreos and chips. Sunshine and Raine are both waiting on Raquel. *Why are they in a group of three?*

"Time to swap roles, the master now becomes the servant, and the servant becomes the master," Dom says.

I look at Leila, waiting for my orders.

"I don't know what to say," Leila says.

"Just say the first thing that comes into your head," I suggest, looking at Leila's blank face.

"Get me a coat, make my bed, scrub the floor with your hair, anything. I know. I have an idea! Why don't we pretend we're in a castle, and I have to defend you, using the broad sword moves I learnt at All Action Inc?"

"Maddie, I'm not sure that's what we're meant to be doing," Leila says.

"Come on! I've been practicing with Dad for years, and now I do sword class as well. We'll do something no one else has thought of, and a knight is a kind of servant," I say. "All I need is a sword."

"Two minutes to go," Dom half sings over all the noise.

"This will do," I say, grabbing a music stand and opening it just enough so I can swing it around without hitting the floor. "You use two hands on a broad sword, raise it up over your shoulder, behind your head then swing it across your body."

As the music stand passes my right shoulder, the legs and shelf come apart, and the upper section clatters into the wall. Everyone turns and stares.

"Oh, no, no, no!" Dom shouts. "You are meant to be miming. Sit down, and see how others have done this."

I sit next to my BF watching other kids demonstrating their work. *It's not fair! Our scene was SO much more interesting.*

Ivan slides closer to us and takes his notes out of his pocket. He has recorded my seven metre leap. *How can I beat the nine metres of a kangaroo hop?*

Dom starts organizing us into small groups. "Stay with the partner you've been working with, but join with another pair.

"Who was your partner?" Dom asks Ivan, who points to George. "Stick together. Imagine you've a giant glue stick, and in these larger groups, I want you to make yourselves into a book. You can only use your bodies. Make sure you have the cover, separate pages, and decide what kind of book you will be — an adventure novel, a picture book, non-fiction. I'll be stepping into your book in a few minutes."

Leila, Ivan, George and I look at each other, as a hum of voices gets louder, and children start moving about.

"The book is easy," I say. "Leila and I can be the cover and you can be the pages."

"We could be *The Ultimate Guide to Winning Hockey,*" Ivan says. "I know all about that."

"Or a Lego manual," George adds.

"What about the *Guru Granth Sahib?*" Leila says.

"The what?" Ivan and George ask together.

"The Sikh..." Leila starts.

"I have an idea!" I jump in. "My dad's often sent a

souvenir book when he finishes a film. We could be the *Cinderella* keepsake, with pages showing us making our film, and winning all those prizes."

"But George wasn't in it," Leila says.

"That's okay, you were at the awards, the after show party, and you'll be in my next film," I promise.

"Just two minutes to go," Dom sings.

The noise in the gym increases as my class sort themselves into the spine, cover and pages of their books.

"Okay, freeze! Now let's see what we've got," Dom says. "Hmm, you can never judge a book by its cover. What's this book about?"

There's SpyCraft: Expert Hints, The Diary of a Total Loser, One Direction, Dare to Dream, and then ours.

"Super idea! I should make a memory book showing the record number of awards *Snow White Meets the Seven Dwarves* got," Dom brags.

Somehow, his compliment makes me feel dreadful. 'Dom the Dude' is talking about the fun we're having, but I just want to go back to our class so I can figure out how to jump nine metres.

"Come, come and sit with me," Dom says. "You are the most creative school group I've ever worked with. You should all come to my acting school. I'd make stars of you all. Now, I have something exciting to announce.

"You...are...going...to put on a play," Dom says. "Each group is going to choose a story, and perform it, live on stage.

"The tale should be one you know well. Maybe it'll be a story you were told when you were little; it may come from the country where you were born, or the place your parents, or grandparents are from. Each group'll be unique. Your Arts grade will be based on the work you put in, and the best work will receive international fame on the 3D Acting for Life website."

"International fame?" Ivan mocks.

I smile, and cover my mouth to stop a giggle bursting out.

"Now, spend the last five minutes in your groups, brainstorming the stories you might tackle."

Ivan, Leila, George and I sit looking at each other.

"Dom, Dom," Raquel calls out. "The Finkles come from Denmark. Can we do *The Little Mermaid*?"

"Excellent idea!" Dom shouts. "Did everyone hear that? This group has already come up with a story. What creativity! Follow their example and we'll have a super show."

Ivan copies Dom the Dude, and I try not to laugh out loud.

"You're just jealous we have an idea, and you don't," Raquel says.

"Oh, we're going to do something way better than *The Little Mermaid*," I say.

"Wanna bet?"

"Yeah! I'll bet we get on his stupid website, and you don't," I say.

"Or what?" Raquel asks.

"I know, whoever gets on the website is the master. Whoever doesn't becomes the servant for a month."

"Oh yes! I'm going to win this. Easy," Raquel says, and we shake hands.

3

MADDIE'S MONKEY KING

"Put your ideas in my hat. The one I pull out'll be the story we try," I say.

It's been a whole week since our class had Drama with Dom the Dude, and we still can't choose the story to perform.

"Can I join in?" Ben asks. "Which animal jumps are we trying to beat today?"

"Yeah! We could do frogs or mountain goats," Ivan says.

"Ivan, we have to choose a story for Drama," I say. "Just think what Raquel'll be like if we turn up with nothing."

"You get Drama. Cool! Grade five sounds awesome!" Ben replies.

I look at him, thinking about our spelling lists, fractions, homework, and Dom the Dude. *Not much that's 'cool' in that.*

I scribble madly, and the others do the same. Then I fold and refold my paper until it's a tiny stiff ball. I take off my black, peaked cap, place my idea into it, and hold it out so the others can do the same.

"We're going to do the story I pull out of the hat. Agreed?" I ask. "Agreed," says Leila.

George nods his head.

"But Russian stories are the best," Ivan insists.

I give Ivan a stern look.

"Oh, come on! I'm the only Russian in grade five, and our stories are full of forests, cannibal witches, and czars getting beheaded. No one will beat that! Or try to copy our idea," Ivan says.

I plunge my hand into the hat and out comes a neatly folded slip of paper. I open it slowly then recognize Leila's curvy writing. I smile at my BF.

"Unfair! Cheat!" Ivan shouts.

I clear my throat and read, "Rama and Sita."

"Who the heck are they when they're at home?" Ivan asks.

"The greatest warrior in all of history, and his beautiful wife," Leila replies.

"I'll be the warrior," Ivan says. "Was he good looking?"

We all pretend to ignore Ivan as he stands in a ninja pose, combing his hair with his fingers.

MADDIE MAKES MONEY   27

"Wasn't the girl stolen by an octopus?" I ask, remembering a reading comprehension we did before Christmas.

"The demon king, Ravana, kidnaps Sita in his chariot," Leila continues.

"Oh! I still have the cart we used for Cinderella. The demon-king-octopus-thingy could put you in that," I say.

"You'll have to be the octopus," Ivan says, looking at George.

"Ravana isn't an octopus. He's a king with twenty arms, and ten heads," Leila says.

"Anyway, just pretend you get taken and put into the cart," I continue, pulling Leila to her feet and handing her to George.

Leila takes off her necklace and throws it onto the icy woodchips.

"What are you doing?" I ask.

"Well, Sita leaves a trail of jewels for Rama to follow," Leila explains.

"Okay, Ivan, you follow the trail. Then what happens?" I ask.

"Rama meets the monkey king, Hanuman, who sends messages to all the animals," Leila continues.

"We've run out of people," George says.

We all look at him.

It's always a surprise when George speaks. It's not that he doesn't talk, but he doesn't chat. He never wastes words, never repeats himself, and I never expect him to open his mouth, so when he does, it takes a moment to process what he's said. As usual, he's right. There are no more actors to be the animals.

"I'll be an animal," Ben says.

"You can't. You're not in grade five," Ivan says.

"No, but our audience could be! I have an idea!" I say. "When I visited my grandma in England last Christmas we went to see *Jack and the Beanstalk*."

"A kids show?" Ivan asks.

"No, a pantomime. They used the audience to tell them where the baddie was. I screamed and screamed, 'He's over there, he's over there, he's behind you,' every time the giant came on stage. So, in our show, you could ask the audience if they've seen Ravana," I say.

Ivan looks unsure, picks up Leila's necklace, stares straight at her, and says, "Have you seen Ravana?"

"Ivan, it only works if you don't look at her. You have to pretend you don't know where she is. You have to work the audience. Watch," I say.

"Oh Sita, Sita will I ever find you? Oh, who are you?" I continue, looking at the audience. "Hello. Will you help me? Oh, I can't hear you. I said, 'Will you help me?'"

"Yeah," Ben says.

"You'll have to be louder," I go on.

"Yes!" Ben shouts.

"Okay, I'll pretend to be Ravana so you can practice," I say. "If you see someone walking like this, shout out, 'Boo! It's Ravana!'"

I walk around with wobbly legs and wavy arms.

"Boo! It's Ravana!" Ben shouts.

"You'll have to be way louder. Let's try again.

"Then as you're leaving the stage, the shopping cart will go across the back, and our buddy class will shout, 'Boo!' And you think they are practicing so you don't look and say, 'That's right. Just shout, "Boo! It's Ravana!" if you see her.'

"That way you get the audience involved," I say. "And all the noise can bring the monkey king, swinging in from the trees.

"What happens after that, Leila?" I ask, climbing onto the rope pyramid, making monkey noises, and swinging from one piece of rope to the next.

"Rama and Hanuman call for all the animals to help them build a bridge," Leila explains.

"Hmmm, how can we do that bit?" I ask. "I know. Ivan and I will bring a gym bench on stage, then run across it, and fight Ravana.

"Dad's been teaching me how to fight for years, and I know some awesome sword moves from my All Action Inc classes. I bet no one else will have stage fighting in their play," I say. "We'll use my dad's swords, but for now let's practice with sticks."

"Maddie, we're not allowed to play with sticks bigger than our fist," Leila reminds me.

"We're not playing! We're working. This is performing arts homework. Unless it looks good, we won't get an A, and you of all people wouldn't want a B on your report, would you?" I say, jumping down onto the woodchips.

"Wow! Awesome jump! I've got to measure that. Could equal a mountain goat," Ivan says.

"What! Come on. We don't have time for your science competition. We have weapons to find," I say.

I make a mental note to leap from higher up next time.

I run into the forest area, closely followed by Ivan and Ben.

"This'll work," I say, picking up a long stick, holding it in two hands and swinging it like a giant axe against a tree trunk.

"Ah!" twin voices scream.

"Who was that?" Raquel squeals, and my enemy emerges from behind a tree, holding her iPad. Sunshine and Raine appear close behind her.

"You're not allowed that," Raquel says, looking at the stick in my hand.

"And you're not allowed that," I say.

"My word against yours."

"Oh! Ignore her," Ivan says. "En garde."

I turn my back on Raquel and shout, "En garde," holding my stick in two hands. "Block my attack. I'll swing for your middle." Ivan turns in defense. The sticks clang together. "Now, I'm going for your legs." Ivan jumps over my broad sword, spinning away from me. "Gottcha!" I shout, slowly moving my stick until it rests on Ivan's neck.

"Zut alors, Madeleine!" Mme Perdu, our duty aid, squeals. "How many times do you need to be told, 'No fighting!'"

I turn to see Raquel clutching her arms around her coat and grinning from ear to ear.

"But this is for..." I start.

"Non! Non! Non!" Mme Perdu shouts. "No sticks bigger than your fist."

"Argh! We can't practice our play without these."

"Zen you'll have to change your play."

Ivan grabs my arm. I throw down my stick and stamp back to the play equipment where Leila and George are sitting, waiting for us.

"We're not allowed to practice the fight," I complain. "How does Mme Perdu think great battles are ever filmed? Everything I've learned from my dad is preparation and practice, 'The Five Ps, Proper Preparation Prevents Poor Performance.'"

"Oh, having trouble with your play?" Raquel says. "What a shame you won't have anything ready for Drama. You could give up and start serving me today."

"Get lost, Raquel," I mutter.

"And Leila, if you want an A, I could ask Dom if you could change into my group. He'll do a special favour for a friend of mine. Come on Team A, let's go, and rehearse our finished script," Raquel says.

"Come on guys, the battle will be the best bit," I say. "Ivan, you'll run towards George. I'll find something high, and jump into the battle as the monkey king."

I climb up two rungs of the rope pyramid and look down. I can see Raquel, Sunshine and Raine watching us from the edge of the basketball court. Raquel is whispering and laughing. *I can leap from higher than this. I've jumped off the old bike shed.* I climb up three more levels and look down. My stomach lurches. I'll have to leap out while gravity pulls me down or I'll get caught in the ropes. *Land it! Land it! Think parkour!*

"Ready everyone!" I shout. "Let's get Ravana!"

"Hang on," Ivan shouts, reaching into his pocket.

"No time!" I yell as the bell tells us that recess is over.

I leap just as Ivan pulls his metal tape measure from

his pocket, lifts it into the air, and thwacks me across my nose. A sharp pain makes me close my eyes, and I land on top of him.

"Maddie's got a boyfriend, Maddie's got a boyfriend," Raquel mocks.

I look up. Warm, sticky drops fall from my nose onto Ivan's face. *I'm bleeding!*

"Argh!" Raquel squeals.

"Incroyable!" Mme Perdu shrieks. "You, boy, go, and clean yourself up. Madeleine, come with me to see Mrs. McIntyre. Everyone else, off you go!"

"I'll see you in class," I say to Leila, hoping my nose will stop bleeding before Drama starts.

4

THE RIGHT IDEA

"Swim 'round the room," Dominic's singsong voice carries to the hallway. "Oh no! Goldfish change directions smoothly, and gracefully. They never bump into each other. Glide like happy fish. Your tank's warm, the sun's shining, and you've just been fed. Now, goldfish can only remember things for a few seconds. When I clap my hands, I'm gonna give you a new emotion, and you'll change the way you move."

Clap. "Angry." Clap. "Excited." Clap. "Sad." Clap. "Frustrated."

I have to go in there. I don't want to but I have to. My nose has stopped bleeding, but the ice pack still stings, and the throbbing continues. *Will I get one or two black eyes from this?*

Clap. "Oh dear, you're in pain."

Everyone fakes sore legs, arms, and stomachaches.

Morgan dives to the ground in an exaggerated death scene. Ivan pretends a bomb has gone off. He jumps backward, collapses to the ground, and lies moaning on the floor.

Clap, clap, clap, clap, clap. "And freeze!" Dominic is red-faced. "I was talking about this girl here."

He points to me.

"Maddie," I remind him.

"Yes, Maggie. Well done, everyone, for staying in character. Now come back to our circle. In Drama we share ideas sitting like King Arthur and the Knights of the Round Table. No one's ideas are better than anyone else's."

"Mine are," Ivan brags.

Mr. Phillips glares in his direction.

"Now, before we get into our groups to start rehearsing our plays, I want you to tell me some of the techniques we can use to put our stories on stage," Dominic says.

He puts flip chart paper in the middle of the circle and stands, holding a Sharpie.

"We have a script," Raquel says.

"Goooood. And when characters talk to each other we call it dialogue," Dominic says, writing 'dialogue' on the paper. "But you can also perform with a narrator."

'Narrator' gets written on the list. *Dom the Dude has really messy writing.*

"Any other ideas?" Silence. Dominic continues.

"There's mime, puppetry, dance... It's about creativity, imagination, hard work, and originality."

I glance at Leila. She's nervous. I can tell. She's holding her hair elastic and fiddling with the shorter strands that have fallen out of her braid. She prefers pen and paper, right and wrong answers, and matrices that show, 'How to Get an A.' I'll need to help her through this.

"I'll be coming around the groups today to make sure everyone is doing a different story. We can't have everyone doing *The Little Mermaid*. Hee-haw!" Dominic brays. "Hard work will be rewarded. Now, move into your groups, and start being creative."

Everyone starts to move.

"Oh, one more thing. Everyone must stay safe. I heard about the lunchtime rehearsal. Full credit for getting together in your own time, but Mr. Phillips and I will be making sure there are no more trips to First Aid."

Everyone laughs, and stares at me.

"This group," Dominic says, pointing at us. "Will have to change their story. Macey, I can't have black eyes and bloody noses in a Dominic Drummond class."

"It's Maddie," I snarl.

"In 3D Acting For Life classes everyone frees their creative spirit, but stays S.A.F.E. safe. Now let's get to work," Dom says.

We sit staring at each other.

"Dom, Dom," Raquel shouts. "We're ready to practice. Look, here's our script."

"Marvelous! Raquel, you're an inspiration! Look everyone. We have a group ready to rehearse on the stage," Dom says.

My enemy glances over her shoulder, forms an L with her index finger and thumb, then mouths "Loser" in my direction.

"We could do a King Arthur story," I say. "There's St. George and the Dragon, The Quest for the Holy Grail, there's one about King Arthur traveling to an island. The king's challenged to a wrestling match by a little Welsh dude, who makes slaves of anyone he beats, and every time King Arthur returns to the island, the wrestling match gets closer and closer."

"I'd beat you every time," Ivan says, jumping on George and getting him into a headlock.

"Ivan," Mr. Phillips warns. "That does not look like Drama."

"But..." I say.

"No buts," Mr. Phillips says. "You heard what Dominic said about staying safe. That does not include wrestling in class."

"Great! Thanks a lot, Ivan."

I look around the hall. I can hear Raquel, Sunshine and Raine stifling giggles. Everyone is working. Notes are being made. Ideas are being tried out, classmates are moving. We're sitting.

"Maddie, what are we going to do?" Leila asks.

"Umm, let me think. I need space. The right idea is just beyond the edges of my brain," I say. "Give me a second. The perfect plan will come to me very, very soon."

"Oh dear!" Dominic shouts. "This is the only group not practicing. Now, there are thousands of stories out there. You only have to pick one. Think of your favourite story from when you were little, and share it with the group."

"What stories were you told?" Dominic asks Ivan.

"Russian ones, of course," Ivan replies. "They're the best!"

"*The Little Snow Girl*'s Russian," Dominic says. "Try that!"

We look at Ivan as Dominic moves towards another group.

"It's such a boring story. There's an old couple who can't have children so they make a girl out of snow, they make her clothes, then she melts, and leaves them," Ivan says.

"I thought 'Russian stories are the best,'" I tease.

"They are if you choose one like *Baba Yaga*, the cannibal witch," Ivan says.

"Eww!" Leila says.

"Cool!" I say. "Let's try it."

"Well, this girl lives near a forest with her father and evil stepmother," Ivan starts. "When her father's out at work, the girl is forced to do all the work around the house."

"You can be the girl, Leila. Let's get up on the stage," I say. "Scrub the floor! Sweep the path! Make my lunch!"

"You can't work up here," Raquel says. "This is our rehearsal space."

"Come on," Leila says.

"No, we have as much right to be here as they do."

"Oh! You have your script ready, do you?" Raquel asks.

"Wash the clothes! Polish the table! Chop the vegetables!" I command.

"Look," Raquel mocks. "They're doing *Cinderella* again. How original."

"It's not *Cinderella*," I say. "It's Ba, Ba, Ba..."

"Ba, ba black sheep," Raquel sings. "Oh, that'll be good."

"Baba Yaga!" Ivan shouts.

"Oh no! Did you just barf?" Raquel asks. "Baba Yaaaagaaaa!"

"Now, this doesn't sound productive," Dominic says. "Raquel's group was here first. You'll have to find another space today."

Dominic moves towards us with his arms outstretched. I look around to see Raquel grinning as we're ushered off the stage. *I hate teachers' pets.*

"Come on," Leila says. "We can practice here. Ivan, what's next?"

"Well, Masha's sent into the forest to get a needle from the stepmother's sister. But before she leaves she wraps a piece of cheese and a bone in a piece of cloth," Ivan explains.

"It's not very exciting," I say.

"Come on! The sister's a child-eating witch who chases Masha through the forest," Ivan replies. "I'll be the cat who tells Masha to get out before it's too late. The dog doesn't say much, so George, you'll be the dog. Then Maddie, you can be Baba Yaga, and chase Leila."

"Are we allowed to run inside?" Leila asks.

"Leila, we're in the gym," I say.

"And Masha gets a head start," Ivan explains.

"Why?" I ask.

"She gives the dog the bone, and the cat the cheese, so they help her," Ivan says.

"But she's a much faster runner than me," Leila says.

"Oh, the cat's gonna be a bit like Inspector Gadget. He gives Masha things to help her get away," Ivan continues. "They're kinda like weapons to give Masha an advantage. You know, like tranquilizer darts in watches, and explosives in pens. Only Masha gets a hankie that changes to a river, and a needle that can grow into thorns."

"Let's try it," I say. "Leila, give Ivan and George the gifts. Then I'll come on as the witch."

I scrunch my face and hunch my back. "Who are you? What do you want?"

"Your sister sent me for a needle," Leila says.

"Now, Baba Yaga tells Masha she has to earn the needle, and sets her to work weaving, while she has a bath," Ivan says.

"A bath? Why would she go, and have a bath? She wants to eat Masha, not wrap her 'snug as a bug in a rug.' And I'm not getting undressed on stage!" I say.

"But it's part of the story," Ivan insists.

"Not in our version, it's not. We'll change that! What happens next?"

"The cat puts a spell on the hankie, and the needle, takes over weaving, and Masha runs out into the forest."

"Okay, let's try it," I suggest. "Leila, run for your life."

"Hang on! The witch has to come back in, find Masha missing, and go ballistic," Ivan continues.

"Finally, I get to do some acting," I say, and turn into the witch. "Where is the girl?"

"Then the witch attacks her cat," Ivan says.

"Oh, my dad's shown me some great fight moves. I can pretend to slap you across the face, like this," I say, showing Ivan the way my open hand moves close to his face as I hit my thigh with my other hand. "Then I'll grab you by the hair, and if you jump to the side, it'll look like I have thrown you across the room. Then I'll run to George, and drive my toe into the floor just next to you, pretending to kick you."

Leila clears her throat. I look up to see Dominic half walking, half running across the room towards us.

"Maisy," Dominic calls.

"I'm Maddie, and it's okay," I say. "We're rehearsing."

"I can't stomach brutality, cruelty, carnage or blood-shed!" Dominic squeals.

"But they're the best bits," I argue.

"No, non, nyet. This is a drama class, not a war zone," Dominic finishes, and flounces away.

"But it could be." I smile.

"Could be what?" Ivan asks.

"A war zone. Our play could be about one of the world's greatest battles, The Battle of Britain, The War of

Independence, *Monsters vs. Aliens*. What's more dramatic than fighting for your life?"

"Yeah! Loads of people had their heads chopped off in the Russian Revolution," Ivan says.

"Gandhi's walk for freedom was pretty exciting," Leila suggests.

"I have the Lego set of The Trojan Wars," George puts forward.

There's a pause while we all take in what George has just said.

"The Trojan Wars!" I exclaim. "Achilles, the Greek Gods, the Trojan Horse, and ten years of fighting. It's perfect!"

"Perfect? For what?" Leila asks.

"This! I'll get to do some stage fighting," I say.

"Maddie, I'm not sure we're allowed to..." Leila moans.

"Come on! We'll all get As! It'll be awesome! We'll practice all the fights in secret so everyone is blown away on the day. What d'you think?"

"I'm in!" Ivan shouts.

"Can we use my Lego?" George asks.

"Um, sure," I say. "Now, let's get started!"

5

CHARGE!

After school, Ivan, Leila, George and I head to Ivan's place.

"Thanks, Mrs. Vladivenski, for letting us practice here," I say, taking off my dripping Gore-tex jacket and stepping over two huge hockey bags sitting by the front door.

"Just be careful. Zis floor can be slippery ven it vet," Mrs. Vladivenski replies.

I sit down on white marble tiles to take off my rain boots. I'm expecting the floor to feel cold, but it's as warm as sidewalks in the sun. *Under floor heating? I've heard of it, but never felt it.* I look around. Ivan's house is enormous. It looks like the five-star hotel we stayed in when Dad was working on a film in Paris. *Where are we going to rehearse?* There are chandeliers in all directions. One light fitting's in an area with an enormous flat-screen TV, surrounded by black leather sofas, and a gold-framed, glass-topped coffee table with various magazines sitting on it. Another's reflected in a huge dining room table. The third light shines over an area cluttered with leather bean-bags, Xbox remotes, another TV, deluxe headphones sitting on a metal stand, wireless speakers, a charging station, multi-coloured cables and two robot dogs. And I'm sitting under the fourth.

"Wow! Your place has changed since the reno," I say. "There's a gazillion things we could break. Let's rehearse in your room."

We follow Ivan up the floating glass staircase and into his bedroom.

Glass cabinets cover two walls, displaying various hockey trophies. Ivan won't speak to me if anything happens to these.

"Nope, changed my mind," I say. "The entrance hall is our best bet."

We turn around and head downstairs.

"If we move these, we can practice here," I say, picking up a kit bag and wheeling it in front of the door.

Leila and George pick up the other bag and stack it on top. I take two wooden swords out of my backpack and stand them against the hockey bags. We pile all our school bags and shoes into a kitbag mountain. I look around at our new stage.

Ivan is leaning over a narrow glass shelf with a bowl of keys, an assortment of sunglasses, and a huge vase filled with lilies and twirly sticks covered in gold glitter. He is arranging his hair in a giant mirror. *The Greek warrior Achilles was meant to be very proud of his good looks. If we can drag him away from the mirror he'll be perfect for the part.*

"Okay, let's get started with the Greek gods protecting Achilles," I say. "Remember, he's held by his ankles, and dipped into a river for protection. So his heels are the only part of his body not made immortal. The only way he can die is by hacking off his feet."

"Ergh! That's gross!" Leila says.

"But it's part of the story. Now, me and George can be the gods. That way, Leila, you'll be ready to be the Greek princess, Helen.

"Ivan, if you do a handstand, we'll catch your legs. Then you can bend your arms so it looks as if we're dipping you into the water."

Ivan stands with his arms raised to the ceiling, places them on the floor, and kicks up his legs. The force makes us stumble backwards. There's a sharp pain across my back as I slam into the gold frame of the shelf. One arm swings out, sending the bowl of keys clattering to the floor. George crumples under Ivan's weight, pulling Ivan's legs over his head until they land on my shoulder. *I can't hold him!*

Then, as if in slow motion, I see Ivan's foot hit the vase. I let go, leap sideways and reach out for the tottering pot. Ivan collapses on top of George, and I land in a heap clutching the vase to my chest.

"Touchdown!" I shout, as water sloshes over my face and neck.

"Iz everyzing okay?" Mrs. Vladivenski calls.

"Fine Mama." Ivan pushes me off him, picks up the keys and places them on the shelf.

I put the vase back on the shelf, and as I'm setting the last lily back, Ivan's mom appears, wiping her hands on a towel. *I could use that towel to wipe my face, and the floor.*

"Ivan, remember, if you break anysing else in zis house, you vill pay for it from your allowance," Mrs. Vladivenski says.

She turns to us with a smile. "Snack vill be ready soon."

Maybe I won't mention the splashes of water just now. I mop up some of the drops with my socks as Ivan's mom returns to the kitchen. *What is it about wet socks and me? I hate wet socks!*

"Wasn't Achilles a baby when the gods dipped him in the river?" Leila asks. "Could we use a doll?"

"Great idea. Ivan, no handstands, we'll use a blond doll. Now let's skip to the moment when Paris, who's Trojan, starts the war by stealing the Greek princess, Helen," I say. "George, see if you can pick up Leila, throw her over your shoulder, and run across the stage."

George looks at me with one eyebrow raised, then walks over to Leila. *If she's small, he's tiny.*

"No, that's not going to work. But I have an idea," I say, running to the pile of bags by the front door. Jumping up, I lean over and grab my backpack. The pile wobbles as I pull out my lunch bag and the spare sweater Mom insists I take to school. Then, near the bottom, I find my pencil case and take out a marker. "Use this as a dagger. We have a Moroccan knife in a silver case at home. Dad brought it back from the Sahara, with a Moroccan princess dress for me."

"A princess dress?" Ivan laughs.

"It's real. It was made for the Moroccan royal family, but the designer decided to give it to me instead. I've grown out of it, but it might fit Leila," I continue.

I leap off the hockey bag tower, and my hair brushes against the hallway's chandelier. I hear a tinkle as the light fitting swings from side to side, and the crystals jingle together. Then there's a thud as one of the school bags tumbles. Leila stands rooted to the spot. *Stay focused on the action!* I grab Leila, hold the marker to her throat and say, "You're coming with me."

"Awesome jump," Ivan shouts. "That might have beaten a grasshopper."

"Ivan, forget about the science competition. We have a play to practice," I say. "And we still have to plan the battle when the Greeks arrive at Troy's city walls, the ten-year siege, and the famous Trojan horse trick that gets the Greeks into Troy to rescue Helen. Can we get back to stealing this beauty?"

Leila and I lie down on the marble floor and pretend to fall asleep. I can feel some water seeping through my pants. *Please don't look as if I've wet myself.*

"Now, creep up to Leila, and hold the marker at her throat," I say.

George follows my instructions in silence.

"You have to say something, or at least look menacing."

George's face looks blank. I grab him by the hand, and pull him back to the front door. Then tiptoeing over to Leila, hold the marker to her throat and whisper, "Don't make a sound, or I'll slit your throat."

Holding the marker in one hand and Leila's braid in the other, we walk backward towards the door.

"This is just like Rama and Sita," Leila says.

"Except that it's a Greek we're stealing. Dad says there're only seven basic stories in the world, and we're doing one of them," I say, turning to George. "Now, you try."

"I won't be as good as you," George says. "Why don't you steal Helen?"

"Then you'd have to be Odysseus, and lead the Greek army to Troy to rescue Helen. You'd be on stage for most of the play, and have tons of lines to learn."

"No, thanks," George says, taking Leila away at marker point.

"That's a start," I say. "We can work on that when the shopping cart has been made into a Trojan chariot.

Now, Ivan, we grab our swords, and declare war on Troy."

I pick up the wooden practice swords, toss one to Ivan and climb onto the hockey bags.

I look down. This is higher than it looked from the floor. *Look out not down. Focus and balance.* Once I reach the top, I hold the sword over my head.

"Stealing Helen is an outrage!" I shout. "We'll travel to Troy, and bring her back, no matter what it takes."

I hear a key in the lock. The door opens a fraction but is met with a wall of bags. Perched high above, I feel my platform shift, then settle again. The others gasp as if I'm about to fall. My stomach reels.

"Oi! Let me in, you little squirt," Ivan's older brother, Stan, calls.

"Hang on a sec," Ivan shouts.

"I'll show you hanging on. I'll 'hang on' to that scrawny chicken neck of yours if you don't let me in."

It's time to move.

Lifting my sword high above my head, I shout, "Taking Helen's an act of war. Charge!"

Behind me, I hear two heavy footsteps followed by a thud against the door. The bags tumble underneath me, and I'm sent flying into the air.

When my feet hit the floor, they land in a puddle of water and continue across the smooth marble. But my upper body stops. Looking up, I see my sword caught in the chandelier. For a second my feet leave the floor. I know what'll happen next, a pendulum swing. I've reached the top. There's only one place for me to go, back where I came from. I fly through the air. *What a classic stunt! How many times has Dad leapt to safety, swinging on a chandelier?*

As I fly back towards the tumbling bags, I catch a glimpse of Leila's horrified face, George squatting on the floor with his arms over his head, and Ivan covering his eyes with his hands.

My feet collide with an enormous hockey bag, which acts like a train buffer.

There's a loud crack.

Suddenly, nothing but air is supporting my upper body. I look up. The whole chandelier is falling. I yank out my sword, roll into a ball and wait.

SMASH!

Crystal beads, glass and metal shatter in all directions.

There's a beat when none of us dare move. We wait, frozen to the spot. *Please let me just press 'Control, Alt, Delete'!*

Instead, Ivan's mom appears.

"Ivan! Vot is going on? My house! You've wrecked my house! Just look at zis! It's ruined! Trashed! Vot you ver sinking of!

"And vot is zis?" Mrs. Vladivenski screams, picking up the wooden sword from the tangle of metal and cables. "Ver you fighting in ze hallway? Durak! You vill have to pay for all of zis."

6

HOW MUCH?

The next morning at school, Leila, George and I are sitting under the climbing wall platform when Ivan comes along, scraping his shoes.

"Hey, what's up?" I ask.

"You," he replies.

"What have I done?"

"I can't have any friends at my house until I pay for the chandelier."

"But when your mom called mine, she said she wanted to check I was okay. All that mattered was our safety," I say.

"Yeah, she might've said that on the phone," Ivan continues. "But with me she went ballistic."

"We'll help," I say. "It wasn't just you. We were all rehearsing. How much do you need?"

"Three hundred dollars," Ivan replies.

"Three hundred!" Leila gasps. "It's going to cost that much?"

"Are you crazy? Chandeliers cost way more, but Dad says I only have to pay something called 'the excess,'" Ivan explains.

Leila sits down on the damp ground and hides her face in her hands.

"Don't worry," I say. "I have ten dollars and forty-nine cents. How much do you have?"

"I can't ask my mom for money. After Ivan's mom called mine, she went to her bedroom, and cried. I tried to make dinner, and found separation papers hiding in the cupboard," Leila whispers.

I give Leila a hug. There's a pain deep in my stomach and a lump in my throat. *What would I do if I found something like that? Mom and Dad don't hide things from me, do they? I'll look when I get home. There're loads of papers lying around.* Leila pulls away from me and wipes a tear from her eye. She's embarrassed, so I turn the attention away from her.

"What about you, George? D'you have any money?"

"Err, I owe money," he stammers.

We all look at him, waiting for an explanation. "I saved up for the Starship Enterprise Lego set, but forgot about the tax. Mom gave in, and paid the extra. I have to pay her back."

"Well, I have two hundred and fourteen dollars and sixty-eight cents," Ivan boasts.

"How did you get that much?" I ask.

"Easy," Ivan continues. "I get ten dollars every time I win a hockey game and five dollars for every goal I score."

We all look at Ivan in amazement.

"Dad says, 'It's motivation.' Professional players earn more if they play well, so why shouldn't I?"

"That leaves..." I clear some wood chips away and write in the soil:

300.00

-10.59

I calculate the answer as quickly as I can. Then continue with:

289.41

-214.68

"Seventy-four dollars and seventy-three cents."

"We can earn that much, and give your mom the three hundred dollars when she comes to see the play," I say.

"Easy. Three weeks, three games, three wins and three goals each game," Ivan says.

"Easy? Let's not count on that," I say. "I have an idea! We could have a lemonade stand."

"In February?" Leila asks.

"Come on. It'll be fun," I say, just as the buzzer sounds for the start of the school day.

When Saturday morning arrives, I'm lying in my nice

warm bed, imaging money clinking into our jar. I can hear Mom and Dad talking in the kitchen. *If they're up, it must be time for action.* I need to make the lemonade, set up a table, and put up the signs I made last night. ' S.O.S. Lemonade.' 'Free Children from Poverty.' 'Break the Chains of Debt.' *They should do the trick.*

My room is still dark. *There aren't many hours of daylight at this time of year. I have to make the most of every minute.* Clambering out of bed, I pull back the curtains to check the weather. White covers our yard like frosting. *Snow! Brilliant! Everyone will get really thirsty shoveling paths, cars and driveways.*

Clothes on. Scrape back my long, curly hair and put it in a ponytail. *All chefs have to make sure hair doesn't get into their food and drink.* Race down the hallway.

"Come on," Dad pleads.

"That's way more than we can afford," Mom says.

"What can't we afford?" I ask.

"Nothing," they say together.

Out of the corner of my eye, I see them look at each other, and then some papers. Dad picks up the pile, and shoves it in a drawer, as Mom walks out of the room. *They do hide stuff. And what can't they afford? If I sell loads of lemonade, I can repay Ivan's mom, then help my mom and dad.*

I take a bag of lemons from the fridge. Cutting board. Knife. Lemon juicer. Sugar. *Time for action!*

The electric juicer whizzes, and I catch most of the

juice in a plastic cup before pouring it into a pitcher. It doesn't look more than a splash at the bottom, so I continue cutting lemons and squeezing.

"Any reason for this sudden burst of entrepreneurship?" Dad asks.

"We were talking at school about families, and money, and how hard life can be. Do you know there're children who have to work so their families can eat?"

"Life can be pretty tough," Dad says. "But why so early?"

"Don't want anyone to steal my idea."

"Princess, I'm sure no one else will have thought of a lemonade stand in February."

"But everyone'll get thirsty shoveling snow."

"For sure. You've spotted a hole in the market. I'll get dressed, clear the path, and help you set up."

I watch Dad leave, and check the hallway is empty before I move to the drawer. *Should I open it?* I reach out my hand, then freeze. *Come on, how bad can it be?* Mom's footsteps make me jump, and I return to my mixture. *I'll investigate the drawer later.*

Before long, the lemonade stand is ready. I look up and down the street. No one. All I can hear is the scritch-scratch of Dad's shovel.

It's just too tempting. I bend down, and roll snow in my hands. It's perfect! Not slushy, not icy, just great, sticky snow. I take aim and throw. The snowball hits Dad right between his shoulders.

"It's like that is it?" Dad says, resting the shovel against the stairs, then making an enormous snowball.

"Snowball fight!" Ben shouts.

Where did he come from? He must have radar which signals 'fun.' Was he watching me doing all the setting up?

Snowballs fly around the yard until we finally take a breather.

"D'you want some lemonade?" I ask.

"Sure," Dad and Ben say together.

"Twenty-five cents," I say.

Dad puts a quarter into the money jar.

"I'll pay you after I've cleared our path. I'm getting paid one dollar," Ben boasts.

I have an idea!

I run to the garage and grab my snow shovel.

"Ben, if we work together we'll do the job much quicker. We can clear your path, then the Dixons, and work down the road. I bet we'll get ten bucks before Ivan arrives."

Shoveling snow is hard work. Ben starts at the house end of his path, and I'm near the road. Scoop. Throw. Shovel. Toss. *There's got to be a better way than this. Of course, it's perfect, sticky snow.* I make a snowball and roll it. As the sphere gets bigger, the path gets clearer.

"Ben, let's make a snowman to hold the lemonade signs," I say.

"Cool!" Ben says, falling into the snow and laughing. "Cool! Get it! It's snow."

I copy him, making a giant snow angel. *No! This won't do.* I stand, and shake snow out of my hair. *Come on! There's no time for kids games. We have some serious money to earn.* I push my snowball along the path. Snow sticks to it, and the snowman base grows bigger and bigger. Ben is working in the opposite direction. His snowball will make the perfect middle.

"Can I play?" Sam asks.

"Sure, start making the head."

Soon we are ready to push our creations across the street and construct our advertising stand. I've never noticed how far it is from Ben and Sam's house. We make it and pause to catch our breath.

The giant snowballs are too tempting. I jump over the smallest ball, leapfrog over the next, and push the largest with all my might into position, next to the lemonade stand. Ben and Sam copy me. Soon the snowman is ready to hold our signs.

"Y'know snowballs make great parkour obstacles," I say.

"Parkour! Parkour! Parkour!" Ben and Sam chant.

"Okay, let's set up a course," I say. "We can come back to the lemonade when there're more people around. Start rolling some new snowballs, and follow me. Dad, call me when customers arrive."

In the back yard, the trampoline has a neat circle of snow sitting on it. Ben, Sam and I clamber on, then jump and kick until the trampoline is clear.

"Try a star jump from here to the ground," I say. "You can place one foot on this snowball, and spin in the air. We can do a belly slide, and forward roll off this one, and with the last, try jumping over it in whatever way you want. I'm going to do a three-sixty."

These jumps take us across the yard, toward the house. There, in front of me, are the climbing-wall features Dad covered our garage with last summer.

"Climb up these, and swing your legs over the patio railing," I say.

The patio has freshly fallen snow covering the table and chairs. I look around to see Ben's head poking over the patio railing.

"We could skate over here," I suggest, pointing to the table. "Then we have to find an exciting way down."

There are the wooden stairs, but I remember just how painful stair falls are. I can see why Dad only does them when he's paid a lot of money. I could slide down the railings, but the risk of slivers is too high.

Then, I have an idea! We could jump from the patio to the front yard. I look down. Surely it's no higher than the bike shed at school. We just need something to break our fall. *Dad's mini trampoline and crash mat.* We could set them up and have a spectacular end to our parkour run.

I race through the house to open up Dad's store, and see Mom in her teaching clothes.

"Mom, it's Saturday. Why are you wearing work stuff?"

"There's a new tutoring business looking for people to work part-time," Mom says. "I'm going along to have a chat with them. Dad'll be here, but it looks as if you're so busy you won't miss me."

I freeze. My heart and brain are racing. *More work? Mom can't need more work, unless...unless we're in debt. Oh, I wish I knew what those papers said. I don't need money for Ivan. I need it for us!*

"Are you okay?" Mom asks.

"Sure," I lie, turning away from her and running into the garage.

As I open the door, Mrs. Vladivenski's car is pulling up in front of the house. *Why did I say I'd help Ivan? It's my mom who needs the money.* I turn my back and pick up the small trampoline. *Perhaps Ivan earned five, even twenty dollars this morning.* I glance over my shoulder. *No, none.* Ivan climbs out of the car with his long, 'we lost' face. I wait until Ivan's mom drives away and struggle across the yard.

"Did you score?" I ask.

"Nope, I would've, their defense was rubbish, but Coach had me on the bench for half of the game," Ivan moans, picking up the money jar and shaking the quarter from side to side. "I see you're doing well."

"Forget that! I've a better idea. Kids are going to pay

me to teach parkour! I'll earn a fortune. Watch this," I say. "If we set up the trampoline, we can fly to the crash mat."

"Where's your dad?" Mom asks.

"Clearing Mrs. Green's path," I reply.

"Just make sure you ask before you use his equipment," Mom says.

"Aren't you going to say bye to him?"

"He's busy," Mom says. "I'll be back before you know it."

I smile at her as I pull out the metal legs of the trampoline.

"See you later," I call, but inside I am panicking. *I know I don't need Mom around all the time, but why does she need SO much work. And why isn't she saying bye to Dad. Have Mom and Dad stopped talking? I've got to do something. I'll earn money, and loads of it, now.*

Ben starts jumping up and down on the trampoline bed.

"It's my turn," Sam whines.

"We could beat our longest jump with this. Grab a tape measure, Maddie," Ivan says.

I run back into the garage, pull out a tape measure, and drag the crash mat into position. When I get back, the boys are taking turns running through the snow, jumping onto the mini trampoline, and flying through the air. When Ivan finally stops, he's three metres and forty-seven centimetres from his take-off point.

"Bet you can't beat that," Ivan brags.

"What d'you bet?" I ask.

"Five bucks."

We shake hands on the deal. *Now what was that science lesson about forces? For every action there is an equal and opposite reaction. So if Ivan jumped three metres and forty-seven centimetres when he jumped from the ground, I should travel with greater force if I jump from a higher point.*

I drag the mini tramp under the patio railing. Then I measure three metres and fifty centimetres across the yard, place the crash mat carefully, and look at my landing area. Everything is set for the challenge.

I climb the wooden stairs to our front door, walk along the landing, and stop at the edge. I look down; my stomach feels like jelly being flipped. *I'm going to do this!*

"I bet kids'll pay a dollar a jump," I say.

"Hang on," Ivan shouts. "I'm getting this on camera."

He takes his phone out of his pocket, runs behind the lemonade table, rests the phone on the tabletop, and gets ready to film.

"Three, two, one, action!" Ivan yells.

I jump, keeping my eyes on the trampoline, but my brain is buzzing. *Wait! If Ivan has to pay the whole three hundred dollars, any money I get has to go straight back to him. This is pointless!* I land, feel the surface sink under my feet, and hear the crunch of snow as the canvas touches the ground. Then I take off, catapulted through the air with enormous speed. My arms and legs search for something solid.

The crash mat passes underneath me. Next stop, Ivan, and the lemonade stand.

"Move!" I scream, as my head sinks into Ivan's stomach.

The impact makes Ivan's phone fly out of his hand as my body thumps down on the table. Time seems to move into slow motion. I turn my head to watch the phone fly through the air and land in the lemonade. The table then flips up, sending the pitcher over my head and into the side of the snowman. Ivan slides to the ground with me on top of him. My eyelids close as I check for injuries. *All's okay, no broken bones.*

"Get off!" Ivan yells, pushing me into the snowman.

I open my eyes. First the head, then the body, then the lemonade falls on top of us. We are covered in icy, sticky liquid.

"I think you owe me five bucks," I gasp.

"And you owe me a new phone!"

7

LEGO WARS

Ivan's still mad at me when we have Drama three days later.

"I'd Google the names of the gods who dipped Achilles into the river, but I don't have a phone anymore," Ivan grumbles.

"I tried to fix it," I reply. "But the rice trick didn't work with lemonade, and snow damage."

"Don't worry," Leila says.

She's sounding nearly as worried as the day I told Ivan we'd help him pay his mom back.

"We can look it up later. Let's see if we can get further than the first scene," Leila says.

"Okay, so Leila, George and Ivan, you come on stage as the three gods, and put this baby doll under the blue material that I'll be wafting about so it looks like ripples of water. Then one of you can say something like, 'Achilles, this will protect you from harm. You're now immortal,'" I explain. "The material can stay on stage, and be the sea the Greeks sail across after the Trojans steal Helen."

"But if George and I are gods, how does he steal me in the next scene?" Leila asks.

"Easy," I say. "The gods will be giant puppets. You can hide inside them. You'll already have your ancient Greek togas on, so all you have to do is take off the gods, and walk back on stage."

"Oh, and I guess you've got three giant Greek god puppets in your back pocket?" Ivan snarls. "Or are you going to pull them out of your magic hat, along with the money we owe my mom?"

"I'll make them," I say. "And we'll repay your mom. I made one dollar and twenty-five cents before school, and two dollars fifty cents at recess from parkour lessons. At this rate we'll have the money by..."

"Graduation!" Ivan snorts.

Clap. Clap. Clap.

"Oh, I just love the creative energy in this room," Dominic squeals. "It's nearly showtime. We're two weeks away from the BIG SHOW. We'll have a dress rehearsal on the day, before your families arrive, so you can get used to performing on the stage. Now, you've five minutes to plan when you're going to meet up and rehearse. Decide who's going to make, or gather props, and costumes. Remember, the show must go on, and everyone who earns an A will get international fame on the

Dominic Drummond Drama, 3D Acting for Life website."

"Dom, Dom," Raquel calls. "We're ready! Do you want to see what we've done?"

"Marvelous! What an inspiration!" Dom cries. "Just five minutes to finish off what you're rehearsing. And remember we don't say, 'Good luck' in the theatre, we say, 'Break a leg.'"

"We need rehearsal time," I say. "Who's free this afternoon? You can come to my house."

"Count me out. I've got hockey," Ivan says.

"I don't think I'll be allowed," Leila says. "Mom gives me strange looks whenever I mention you. Then she goes on and on about the chandelier, and how I could've been hurt."

"Then it'll have to be at your place George," I decide. "Let's go to the office so we can phone home, and tell our parents."

I ride my skateboard the long way to George's house and wait at the corner. George and Leila both climb out of Mrs. Choudhury's car, closely followed by Leila's mom. I can't quite hear the conversation at the door. Eventually, Leila goes into George's house, and I watch her mom drive away. *This is so unfair! The chandelier was an accident. Am I the only person who sees that?* I wait a minute to check the coast is clear. Then ride to the back door, where George is waiting. We walk into the kitchen together. Mrs. Papadopoulos and George's grandmother are sitting drinking tea. They look from George to Leila and me, eyebrows raised, waiting for an explanation.

"We're going to practice our play like I told you. Mom and Gran, this is Maddie. You met Leila and her mom at the door," George says to the stunned grown-ups. "We need my Trojan War Lego set."

George sets off, and we follow awkwardly. Behind us, the two women burst into rapid, machine gun fire Greek. I look around to see arms waving, and pointing in our direction. Then George's gran stands up and follows us.

"Are they okay about us practicing here?" I ask.

"Ignore them," George says.

We look from George to his gran.

"I didn't mention that the friends coming over are girls, and I've never had any girls in my room. Well, I've had my sisters, cousins, aunts, mom, and grandmothers of course, but they think this is different."

George's grandmother pushes past us, opens the door, enters, and sits on a chair in the corner.

"She'll just sit," George says. "She doesn't speak much English, and she'll probably fall asleep in a minute."

I stand at the doorway with my mouth open wide. George's room is ALL Lego. The curtains, bedcover, pillowslips and rug all have bright Lego bricks printed on them. The walls are covered with Rubbermaid stacking shelves with hundreds of plastic boxes all labeled with Lego parts — 'Yellow Bricks,' 'Red Bricks,' 'Black Bricks,' 'Wheels,' 'Plates,' 'Figures,' 'Weapons,' 'Doors and Windows' and 'Plants.' On and on they go, and every surface's covered with completed models. The Starship Enterprise sits on a table beside his Lego bedside light. On top of the shelves there sits a fire engine, ambulance, search and rescue helicopter, R2-D2, an X-wing Starfighter, the Parthenon, Coliseum and Hogwarts, all made out of Lego.

Then, there on his desk sits The Trojan Wars set, complete with the walls of Troy, Greek battleships on a blue Lego sea, tents, soldiers, weapons, and a temple on the yellow sand, the gods watching from Mount Olympus, and an enormous model of the Trojan horse with soldiers hiding inside.

"George, this is brilliant," I say. "We can use this to write the script. Quick, Leila, get some paper and a pen. This won't take long at all."

Leila sits near the desk, resting some paper on her homework binder, I move to the gods, and Mrs. Papadopoulos Senior covers her legs with a Lego blanket.

"We'll open on the three gods, protecting the baby doll, Achilles, from harm," I say. "Then I can walk across the stage with a sign saying 'Twenty Years Later.' That should give you and George enough time to take the god puppets off, and be ready for Helen's capture.

"Let's put these soldiers to one side, and use four Lego

figures to be the four of us," I say, rummaging in the Rubbermaid box for pieces that look like Leila, Ivan, George and myself. "Models are great for planning. My dad uses model cars every time he plans a car chase. He flips them, skids them, even smashes them. That way they wreck fewer real cars. This may even stop us having accidents.

"Okay, so here you are, Leila, lying asleep as Princess Helen," I continue. "Then George, you'll come in, put my Moroccan dagger to Leila's throat and say, 'You're coming with me!' You'll force Helen into a Trojan ship, that I'll make from the shopping cart, and you'll wheel Leila across the stage to Troy."

"How will people know the difference between Greece and Troy?" Leila asks.

"Easy! We'll have signs, 'Greece' on one side of the stage, 'Troy' on the other with the material sea between them," I explain. "Next, Ivan and I'll come on stage as the Greeks, Odysseus and Achilles. We'll declare war: 'Stealing Helen is an outrage! We'll travel to Troy and bring her back. No matter what it takes!'

"We'll then do the battle scenes in slow motion, starting with huge broad sword moves, then toga and dagger fighting, and bare-knuckle fighting. After each clash you and George can count the years. 'The Trojan War went on for one year...two years...three years.' Ivan and I will pretend to get more and more tired until you say, 'Ten years went by.' Then George, you'll come on stage and kill Achilles."

"Isn't he immortal?" George asks.

"No, the gods held him by the ankles so he's not protected there," I say. "Slice Ivan's feet off. Then drag him along until he bleeds to death."

"I can't carry Ivan," George says. "He's too heavy."

"Then we'll put him on my skateboard. You can pretend to drag Achilles across the stage. Then Ivan can trail red ribbons behind him. That'll be the blood gushing from his body."

Leila and George give each other a look.

"Come on. We're nearly at the end. I can talk to Achilles' dead body, saying something like, 'We've been here for ten years. The soldiers are tired, and just want to go home. You're with the gods, please ask for their help to end this war.' Then I'll get the idea to build a statue of a giant horse, and hide soldiers inside its body. We'll give it to the Trojans. When the horse is taken into the city, the Greek soldiers will kill everyone, and rescue Helen.

"There're going to be loads of costume changes, voices from offstage, and signs to make. We just need a way to build the Greek battleships, and the Trojan wall."

I lie back on the Lego rug and stare at the Lego curtains. Mrs. Papadopoulos Senior is snoring quietly in the corner. The room is getting dim. Days are so short at this time of the year. Leila's mom'll be here soon. Leila is looking at me, pen in hand. *I need an idea, and I need it now! Just one bit left to plan, and we'll be guaranteed an A. Come on! Success has worked on Mrs. Choudhury before. She liked me again after I won Best Film Action. Now we need an A so Leila's parents will stay together, and I'll keep my BFF. Think! Why do ideas stop flowing just when you need them most?*

I roll over, turn on the Lego bedside lamp, and spin it towards Leila and her notes. The room lights up. Great shadows of the Trojan battlements fall on the wall behind the desk.

"That's it!" I shout, waking Grandma with a start. I push George's Lego bedcover to the floor and rip the sheet from his bed. "Shadow puppets! We can fill in the action with Lego shadow puppets."

I tuck the sheet into the head-high Rubbermaid boxes and move the lamp into position. "Look what happens when the Greek warship passes the light."

A huge shadow of the model passes across the white backdrop. Mrs. Papadopoulos Senior smiles, and claps her hands.

"We can do the same with whole legions of soldiers. And battles could start behind the screen using shadow puppets, then Ivan and I could continue on stage. We could show some of the horrors of war, heads can be cut off, and blood can spurt out. We could even see the Greeks building the Trojan horse, then the real thing'll come on stage for the finale," I say, demonstrating Lego shadow puppets.

Everything is fitting into place. My brain is buzzing, and my whole body tingles. It's hard to speak fast enough. My arms and legs make huge movements as I demonstrate the live battles. My voice is getting louder as I rip heads off the model soldiers and bring their swords clashing onto minute shields. There is a gasp as I break the legs off the Trojan horse and hold them in front of the lamp.

"It's going to be brilliant!" I yell, as the doorbell rings. "We'll all get As, and your mom'll let you play at my house."

"Shhh, Maddie!" Leila panics. "I have to go."

"Sure, we'll practice at school," I whisper, giving my

BF a hug, and fighting imaginary Trojans until I hear the front door close.

"Thanks Mrs. P, thanks Grandma P and thanks George, your Lego set is the best," I say, racing out of the back door.

I leap on my electric skateboard, pretend I'm part of a cavalry charge as I fasten my helmet and set off for home.

I love it when ideas seem to tumble from my brain. No sooner does one scene start than another notion pops up. It's like watching our play in fast forward. Giant gods, shadow puppets, live fights, bloodstained soldiers and – victory. Nothing can stop us from being the best.

I jump up, high-five a lamppost, and stop. A poster, stapled to the wood, catches my eye. There're pictures of Batman, Mulan, Wolverine, Elastigirl, Luke Skywalker and Princess Leia on the small notice. I read on. 'Who is your hero? Write a description, record a video, or draw your hero in action. Enter the Blood Services Canada's competition: Be A Hero – Give Blood. Win a place in a national advertising campaign.'

A national ad campaign! Dad always earns loads of money when he films commercials. If I win this, I'd make enough to pay back Ivan's mom, buy him a phone, and help Mom and Dad. They'll stay together, and Ivan'll stop bugging me. No more lemonade stands, waiting to see whether Ivan wins his hockey game, or trying to get kids to pay for parkour. And winning the award at the Young Moviemaker made Mrs. Choudhury like me again. If I win this, then Leila and I could be friends again. Or, y'know, still be friends, but her mom could know.

Heroes? I have to think of something that no one else will do. Heroes? I'm not doing a superhero or a movie character... too many others will try that.

Then it comes to me. Hero! I race home, burst through the front door, and run to my room. The library book of Greek myths is lying open at the Trojan Wars. I pick the book up and flick through the pages. Here it is, the story of Hero and Leander. I read on:

> Hero, a priestess of Aphrodite, lived in a tower on the European side of the Hellespont. Leander, a young man from Abydos, lived on the other side of the strait. Leander fell in love with Hero and would swim every night across the Hellespont to be with her. Hero would light a lamp at the top of her tower to guide his way.
>
> These visits lasted through the warm summer and slowly Hero fell in love with Leander's soft words.

Ergh! Gross! We'll leave that bit out! But the picture of a wild storm, a drowning body, and a woman jumping from a tower makes me read on.

> One stormy night, the waves tossed Leander in the sea and the wind blew out Hero's light; Leander lost his way, and was drowned. When Hero saw his dead body,

she threw herself over the edge of the tower to her death
to be with him.

*That's it! We have the Greek costumes, and the blue
material for the sea. I've almost finished the Aphrodite and
Poseidon god puppets. Aphrodite could get jealous when
Hero falls in love with Leander, and Poseidon can brag
about putting an end to it. Perfect! This is going to solve all
my problems. What could go wrong?*

8

TOO MANY HEROES

"Morning everyone," Mr. Phillips says, the next day at school. "I've something exciting to announce."

I look up. *Why do teachers use the word 'exciting' when they actually mean they have a load of extra work for us?*

"Blood Services Canada want people to know that we can save a life by giving blood. That's pretty amazing. So they're asking us about the heroes in our lives, and tell the world what makes them incredible. You can put your ideas into a poem, letter, song or film," Mr. Phillips explains.

My stomach sinks. *This was my idea.*

George's hand shoots into the air.

"Yes, George you can do stop motion animation, if that was going to be your question," Mr. Phillips says.

Everyone laughs. George's face goes red. I stop

writing my note to Ivan and shove the paper inside my desk. *Now, I not only have the whole of Canada to compete with, I have my class as well.*

"There are so many ways to present an idea creatively. Raquel's drama group are recording an old David Bowie hit, 'Heroes,' as we speak. It may end up as the theme tune for the campaign. Who knows?" Mr. Phillips continues.

"Ergh! My day just gets better and better," I grumble.

"Now, let's brainstorm what a hero is," Mr. Phillips says, whiteboard pen in hand.

"Batman," Morgan yells.

"Spider-Man," Stu says.

"Well, they're superheroes. But what qualities do they have that humans without super powers can have?"

"They're strong," Morgan yells.

"Yes, but don't forget to put your hands up if you have an idea. Yan Yan?"

"They're brave."

"Excellent! A hero is someone who's brave, and inspires us to be a better person. Now working with the person next to you, finish this spider chart. See if you can fill a page with ideas about who your hero is, and why."

"Who's your hero?" I turn and ask Leila.

"You, I guess," she says.

"Come on, it's got to be someone who's done amazing things like Batman, Catwoman, Barack Obama or my dad."

"And me," Ivan brags.

"Ivan, I've an idea that's going to win us this competition, get us on TV, and earn us loads of money," I say, grabbing the note from my desk and handing it to him. "But don't talk about it in class. This has to be a secret."

"Well, I guess my mom's my hero," Leila confesses. "She came to this country, not knowing anyone. Now she has a home, family, job, and loads of friends."

"Yes, that works," I say. "I can write about my dad. He's got to be brave to do all his crazy stunts and I want to grow up to be just like him. Wouldn't that be amazing?"

"When you've filled your paper," Mr. Phillips says, "you'll need to decide how you're going to present these ideas. It could be a letter to your hero explaining why you admire him or her; it could be a poem, a song or an animated story. The choice is yours. Take five minutes to start planning your project. We'll all have something ready for the performance of Stories from Around the World, and the best will be sent off to Blood Services Canada."

There's a groan as we all turn our heads from our teacher to the papers in front of us. *If I edit Dad's work with some of my own stunts I can show the world how like him I am, one clip of him, then one of me. I bet he'll know a cheesy song that I can set it all to, or better still, I can write my own voice-over. I'll remind Mom how brilliant Dad is. Then, after the show, I'll make dinner while they go for a walk, and fall in love all over again. Perfect!*

I draw a line down the centre of my page, head one

column 'DAD' and the other 'ME.'

DAD	ME
Stair fall from show reel	Cinderella stair fall
Knight's duel	All Action Inc broad sword class
Motorbike wheelie	Wheelie on mountain bike — better get practicing
Titanic fall into water	Hero's plunge to save Leander
Running from burning building	??????

Hmmm! How can I get a shot of me on fire? Dad's fire suit will be way too big for me. And he says I'm too young for body burns.

Raquel, entering the classroom, interrupts my thoughts. And when I say entering I mean a full-on stage entrance with hair being flicked from her make-up covered face. *I thought Mr. Phillips said they were recording a song. So why does Raquel need make-up? No one is going to see her face!*

"Morning, Raquel," Mr. Phillips says. "How was the recording session?"

"Amazing!" Raquel squeals. "The song sounded incredible. And there was a film crew. The news reporter interviewed me. You'll probably see me on TV tonight."

"Sounds like quite an experience," Mr. Phillips says. "It's going to be hard to come down to earth after a morning like that. Sunshine and Raine will fill you in on our Heroes project. I'm sure you will have lots to contribute."

Raquel flounces to her desk, sits down and starts whispering to her fan club.

"If Raquel gets onto TV and I don't, we'll never hear the end of it," I say to Leila.

"Don't worry about her, I need your help. I hate it when we're told we can work in whatever way we want. I never know where to start," Leila says.

"It's easy," I say. "Start with a thought like, 'My mom's my hero,' dress her in a Wonder Woman costume, start a comic with her doing normal stuff like getting you to school then when there's been an accident closing the bridge, have her fly over the traffic.

"Oh, she could use her killer looks as laser vision to put a force field around you so you never get hurt. You could even give her a background, 'Her parents knew she was no ordinary child when she picked up a sacred cow, and carried it off the road.' She can pick up cars to find a lost teddy, stretch her arm from the kitchen to the driveway to help you rollerblade, and clean the house using supersonic breath control to blow all the dirt straight into the bin while making the beds and loading the dishwasher."

"Yeah," Leila says. "I never thought of it like that."

I'm scribbling madly when the bell rings for recess. *Argh! I've spent the whole time drawing cartoons, and making suggestions for Leila.* My 'Hero' creation will have to go on my homework list.

I grab Ivan's arm.

"I need to tell you about Hero and Leander," I say. "We're going to film the story, and send it to Blood Services Canada in secret."

"No way. I have hockey, the science competition, that stupid play, this project, and my mom going on and on about the money I owe her," Ivan replies.

"But don't you see, this'll be the answer for everything. Hero jumps from her tower to save Leander. That's your mountain goat leap. The story's another Greek myth so we can use the same gods and costumes we're getting ready for *The Trojan Wars,* and it's for a national ad so we'll get loads of money," I say.

"Loads of money? For what?" Raquel interrupts.

"None of your busi–" I start.

"Maddie's entering us into the Hero competition," Ivan answers.

"You! You haven't got a hope. We went to a professional recording studio, and there's no guarantee we'll be used. Although, we did sound awesome," Raquel brags. "What are you planning? Another home movie?"

"Our 'home movie' happened to win Best Editor, and Best Movie Action, in case you've forgotten," I say.

"And we won, let me see, Best Actor, Best Costume Design, Best Music, Best Cinematography and, I think there was one more, let me see if I can remember, oh yes, Best Movie," Raquel boasts. "You're an amateur, admit it."

"I bet we can do it," I say.

I can feel my face burning, and Leila's long fingers stroking my back, trying to calm me down.

"Okay, I'll take that bet," Raquel says, holding out her hand. "Ten dollars says you're not in the advert."

I grab her hand and shake it. Raquel turns on her heels, grabs Sunshine and Raine by the arms then says in a voice loud enough for me to hear, "Fools and their money are easily parted."

"Come on," I say to Leila and Ivan. "We'll show her."

9

3, 2, 1, ACTION!

"TV ads are really short," I explain while carefully painting Aphrodite's face onto a burlap sack. Leila and Ivan are gluing long strands of matted wool onto another sack for Poseidon's hair, and George's arranging his Trojan Lego wall beside us. "We won't film them falling in love. I'll fill these sacks at home, and dress the gods in sheets. Then we can have Aphrodite and Poseidon arguing. Aphrodite can say 'Ergh! A priestess in love! That's gross! This can't go on! Let's put a stop to it.' Then we'll see Leander swimming, the sea getting rougher, Leander drowning, and Hero jumping to his rescue. Look, I've got it all planned out."

I unfold a piece of paper with the scenes listed in order.

"Where am I going to swim in February?" Ivan asks.

"We'll use your hot tub," I reply.

"Except that I have a 'no friends over to play at my house' rule, thanks to you," Ivan grumbles.

"We'll find a way," I say.

"Shouldn't we just focus on the play?" Leila suggests.

"Come on! We need the money. I promised I'd help Ivan pay his mom back. We have the costumes, and I can't lose the bet with Raquel. Where is she anyway?" I say.

I look across the gym to *The Little Mermaid* rehearsal. Sunshine's in tears. There's no sign of Raquel, so I walk over to check out what's happening.

"I can't do it," Sunshine cries. "Raquel is SO much better than me."

"Of course, Raquel is better. Hee-haw. She's been studying with me for years," Dom brays. "Darling, you only have to read Ariel's lines today, so the group can rehearse. Anyone can read. It's not as though we're looking to replace your star. Here, even Mini can read the lines for you."

"It's MADDIE," I say through gritted teeth. "Where's Raquel?"

"She left early for a catalogue photo shoot," Raine says.

"And this is our last chance to rehearse in class before the show," Sunshine sobs. "We can't do it without Raquel."

"Yes you can," I say. "Just remember Cinderella. You did that without Raquel. And you still have a week 'til the show. There'll be loads of time to practice."

Sunshine and Raine look up at me with big, scared eyes.

"Will you help us?" Sunshine asks.

I look over my shoulder. Ivan and Leila are busy making Poseidon, and the Legos are taking an age to put together. Reaching out my hand, I take the script, and look for Raquel's first line.

"Marvelous! Rehearse with Ariel's understudy today, and you'll have the real star back in no time," Dom says, flouncing away to another group. "Now, how's my little Chinese story coming along?"

Sunshine and Raine give me a hug. I mouth, "Sorry" to my group. Now I'm stuck rehearsing my enemy's part, in my enemy's play while she earns the money I need. Great. My television debut has to happen now.

After school, Ben, Ivan and I get together at my place. The whole day has seemed grey and dark, but I'm determined to film something for this competition.

"I can't have one of my priestesses falling in love. Hero has broken her vow of serving me," I say, holding the Aphrodite puppet over my head, and looking out across our front yard. "Poseidon, you have to help me put a stop to it."

"I am all powerful, my authority over the sea is undisputed. All that I command will happen," Ivan says, holding the broomstick, making the Poseidon puppet bob up and down. "Just watch. This love affair will be over in one short raging storm."

"Great. Cut. Did you get that, Ben?" I ask.

"Sure did," Ben replies, holding my iPad out in front of him.

"Fantastic. We'll film the first part of Hero's leap from the tower in a few minutes when the sun goes down. I'll jump from our patio to the mini trampoline. Ivan, that'll be a human attempt at a mountain goat jump," I say, pulling Dad's equipment into place.

Ivan takes his enormous metal measuring tape from his jacket pocket and calculates the distance from the patio railing to the ground.

"Fifteen feet. Mountain goats jump fifty feet. All this shows is animals are better than humans at jumping, and that's been obvious all along," Ivan moans.

"Well, you could show the jump in slow motion to make it look higher than it is. Dad uses that camera trick all the time. And hello... I could do with some help over here," I say, trying to pull the enormous crash mat across the yard.

Ben runs to my assistance, and Ivan reluctantly puts the measuring tape away.

"Once we're done here, we'll use your hot tub for the drowning scene," I say.

"What time does your mom get home?" I ask.

"I dunno. Somewhere around five," Ivan replies.

"Come on then, let's get into our costumes. We don't have much time."

We run inside, and I spread a sheet on the floor. Ivan and Ben help to roll me up into it, but I look like a beluga whale washed up on a beach. I can't even stand up on my own.

"It's got to be looser or I won't be able to climb onto our patio railing."

I wriggle out and try draping the sheet over my shoulder, wrapping the extra material around my waist then back over my other shoulder. It doesn't look like the pictures in my book, but the sheet covers my black swimmers and shorts. *Making togas is harder than it looks. We'll have to practice before the play next week.*

Once I'm in my costume, I help Ivan drape another sheet over his designer jeans and Canucks sweater.

"Watch the hair!"

"Come on," I say. "We have to get on with this, or your mom'll be back before we get to your place."

That makes Ivan move. We shuffle outside. I feel the cold air on my bare arms. *I should've put my ski thermals under the toga.*

"Do you think the gods should look on?" I ask.

"Definitely," Ivan says. "Those Greek gods are such busybodies. They keep sticking their noses into other people's business."

"Grab a plant pot," I say. "We can poke the puppet

sticks in the dirt, then Aphrodite and Poseidon can watch in the background as I leap to save Hero."

Ben and Ivan drag our potted Christmas tree into position. Then I ram the broomsticks, holding the puppet gods, into the hard-packed soil. Aphrodite and Poseidon loll apart. They look as if they'll fall, so I prop them against each other and support them with the snow shovel.

I stand back to check the scene, hold up my fingers to make an imaginary screen, raise my arms to my launch position, and imagine the camera following my fall.

"Move the pot a little bit that way," I say, pointing to the house. "And we'll definitely get those troublemakers in the shot. Oh, just one more thing. We need Hero's lamp, to guide Leander as he swims."

I run inside and come back a few minutes later with a candle, strike a match, and set it burning. I climb onto the railing and look down at Ivan, standing in his toga holding the iPad, and Ben standing beside him. It's harder to see the mini tramp in the fading light than it was in the snow. My stomach flips over and does a jello dance inside me.

"Come on, Maddie. Hurry up or my mom'll get home before we're done," Ivan says.

"I'm ready. Ivan, is the camera rolling?" I ask.

"Rolling!"

"Then, three, two, one, action!" I yell, taking a giant leap from the patio.

"No! Stop!" Ben cries. "You're on fire!"

"Fire? What fire?" I shout.

Somewhere above and behind my head I can see a flame. *I AM on fire!* The piece of material flung over my shoulder must have touched the candle. I grab the sheet and hold the flames away from my body as I fall. *Keep calm!* I think as the mini tramp launches me back into the air.

"Help! This'll burn a hole in Dad's mat!" I scream, as I land on the crash mat and take huge running leaps over the squidgy surface. "Get me out of this thing!"

As I unravel, the flames travel along the sheet like a

dynamite fuse. "Ivan, you have shoes on. Stamp on the flames!"

Ivan looks down at his new runners, and his toga, and keeps filming. I clamber out of the sheet, drop it on the grass, and run into the garage for Dad's fire extinguisher. *Oh, that's why he has someone standing nearby, on fire safety duty, whenever he's set on fire.* I grab the extinguisher, run back to the burning heap, point the hose towards the flames, and press. White powder is released and blasts me backwards with a great whooshing noise.

"Just what are you hooligans up to?"

We spin around. That evil, sour-faced neighbour, Mrs. Green is standing with her hands on her hips. "Do your parents know what you are doing?"

"It was an accident," I stammer. "It's for a school project —"

"Do I look like I was born yesterday? I've a good mind to report you to the police," Mrs. Green shouts, striding down the road.

"Quick, run!" Ivan says. "Let's get to my house."

"We'll need another sheet, and the gods," I call, checking the smoldering heap of cloth lying on the grass. *The fire is out. No danger there, but who knows about Mrs. G.* I run inside, grab another sheet from the linen cupboard, throw a sweater over my swimsuit and shorts, and return Dad's extinguisher to its home in the garage.

When I come outside, Ben and Ivan are already running down the road, with the gods slung over their shoulders. There's a trail of shredded paper following them.

"Wait up!" I yell. "You've got to be gentle, or the gods will fall apart."

Ivan and Ben don't even turn around. I'm not sure whether they can hear me. I have to catch up, so I jump onto my electric skateboard and press the on switch. *Why can't my ideas follow plan A? Just once.* I think to myself as I speed away from my house in pursuit of my friends.

———

By the time we reach Ivan's house, Aphrodite has lost most of the stuffing from her body, and her head flops to one side. We pull a pot next to the hot tub, set up the gods so they're resting against each other.

"She looks as if the shock of losing a priestess to love has drained every ounce of strength out of her," I say.

The boys ignore me and lift the lid off the tub. Warm steam rises into the cold night air.

"If you jump up and down in the hot tub, and pretend to swim at the same time, it'll look as if you're in a storm. Then say something like, 'Hero, Hero, I have to get to Hero,' then drown. I'll jump in, try to rescue you, but the water will be too rough, and I'll die beside you.

"Ben, make sure you get a shot of the two of us floating in the water, and end with a shot of the gods' faces. Positions everyone."

Ivan climbs into the hot tub. Ben switches on the iPad, then looks for the best place to stand and film. I take off my sweater, wrap the sheet around my body and climb onto the edge of the tub.

"This is going to be amazing," I say.

"Just hurry up," Ivan says. "If I get caught having friends over to my place, I'm dead meat."

"Don't worry. We're the one-shot wonders. Positions. Camera rolling? And action!"

Ivan plunges his head into the water, jumping up and down. Giant waves mix up the clear, steaming water, until it splashes over the edge and onto the deck. His arms are like windmills, making stationary front crawl movements, and each time he lifts his head to breathe, he gasps out Hero's name. *This is awesome!*

Then his arms go limp, and Ivan floats, head down in the turbulent water.

"He's drowning!" I shout, jumping into the water and grabbing Ivan's limp body. "Help! Help! You can't die!"

A scream breaks into the action. Ivan's mom is clattering across the patio in her high heels.

"No! Ivan!" she cries.

Mrs. Vladivenski grabs her son by his toga and yanks him out of the water.

"Get off me!" Ivan shouts. "We're filming!"

There's a beat. Silence. A moment when you can watch panic turn to fury. Blood drains away from her face, hits Mrs. Vladivenski's feet, and bounces back to her head with the full force of an erupting volcano.

"You! You again!" Mrs Vladivenski screams. "Get out! Get out! Get avay from my son! Get avay from my home! I never vant to see you again! Just get out!"

Ben retreats across the yard. I climb out of the hot tub and pick up a god in each hand. *I could do with a towel.* Ivan's mom's face looks like an angry Greek god. *Maybe now isn't the time to ask.*

Ivan races inside.

Mrs. Vladivenski watches me leave in silence. Then she follows Ivan into the house and screams, "Ivan, I sought you ver drowning! How could you be so stupid! You vill be the death of me. And I said 'No friends'!"

"Let's get out of here," I say, jumping onto my skateboard and racing away as fast as the wet toga, my shivering body, and the gods will allow.

How did this film get into such a mess? Every time I try to sort something out, I make things worse.

"Maybe if Ivan's on TV his mom will forgive me," I say. "Come on, Ben. We can edit the advert at my place."

10

THE END?

Plans change the second I walk into the kitchen. Mom and Dad are at the kitchen table with the burnt sheet sitting between them.

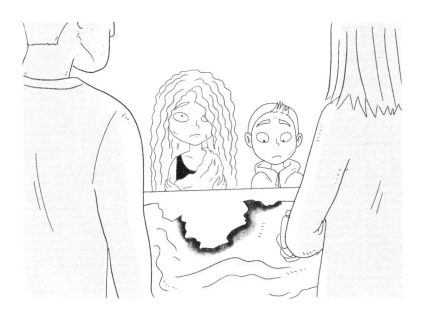

"Mrs. Green stopped by a few minutes ago, and we've had a call from Mrs. Vladivenski. We need a family meeting," Mom announces.

"I'd better go," Ben whispers.

He places my iPad on the table and beats a hasty retreat.

I hate family meetings. They're almost always about me, and one look at my parents' faces tells me we're not about to decide on a vacation.

"How did *this* happen?" Mom asks, holding some scorched material in her outstretched hand.

My thoughts bump, and trip over on all the things I shouldn't mention.

"It was an accident," I mumble.

Mom's and Dad's faces look calm, but unnaturally still, like they are not telling me something. *Are they angry? Disappointed? Will this be the moment that they tell me they are breaking up because of me?*

"An accident? A burnt sheet, a neighbour threatening to call the police, drowning a friend in his hot tub," Mom starts, her calm exterior shattering before my eyes.

"Take it easy," Dad says.

"Easy! How easy will it be if Maddie really hurts herself or a friend?" Mom shouts. "What were you thinking?"

"I was trying to win a competition, trying to be just like Dad, and make the judges say, 'Wow!'" I cry. "But I've failed. I've failed!"

"Do you see where Maddie's hero worshipping gets her?" Mom asks.

"No, you can't blame Dad!"

I run to my room, slam the door and bury my head in the pillow. *Why did I mention Dad? Mom's blaming him now. This was meant to show Dad's brilliance, but I've made things worse.*

There's a gentle knock on my door. I don't answer. *Please knock again. Please come in, and tell me it's all going to be okay. Please don't leave me like this.*

Minutes feel like hours.

There's another knock.

"Maddie," Mom says. "Can we come in?"

"Mmm," I cry.

The door opens slowly. I can hear Mom and Dad stepping over the clothes scattered on the floor. Mom rests her hand on the small of my back, and Dad strokes some hair from my forehead. They're both breathing slowly and deeply.

"Maddie, I'm sorry I lost my temper," Mom whispers.

I think she's crying. Mom cries at every soppy movie. Her eyes water up when she hears the violins, but this feels different. This is not a movie. There's no happy ending. I don't want to hear what they're about to say.

"Maddie, we'll find a way to make things okay again," Dad chokes out.

I swing my body around. Throw my arms over their shoulders and weep into Dad's sweater. I can feel snot coming out of my nose. *Do I wipe it on Dad or sit back and find a Kleenex?*

I choose the second option, relax my grip, and accept the tissue Mom holds out like a flag of surrender.

"Are you ready to tell us what's been going on?" Mom asks in her softest, kindest voice.

I take a deep breath and tell them all about the lessons with Dom the Dude. I explain the bet with Raquel. The way we have to be the best so we can get on the website, and I don't have to serve my enemy for a month. *Oh, it feels good to talk about this!* I take another breath that's almost a sob, and continue. I tell them about the rehearsals, the way Mrs. Vladivenski said not to worry about the chandelier, but she's making Ivan repay three hundred dollars, and because Ivan made me feel so bad, I said I'd help. So I tried to get the money with a lemonade stand in February, but we only got twenty-five cents and drowned Ivan's phone.

I tell them about the parkour lessons, Ivan's two hundred and fourteen dollars and six-eight cents, my ten dollars and forty-nine cents, the way Ivan gets paid for hockey wins, and the fifty nine dollars and seventy-three cents we still need.

I tell them about Ivan's Regional Science Competition, and how I've been inventing ways to beat animal jumps, but my ideas have led to a bleeding nose and a school-wide ban on jumping from swings.

I want to tell them I'll solve our family problems, but Dad interrupts me.

"Oh, is that all?" Dad says. "I thought you were going to say you were having problems with fractions."

"Dad!" I half laugh, and hit him on the shoulder.

No matter what happens, Dad always tries to make a joke of it. And I always laugh even when I try not to.

"Wow! That's a lot for one ten-year-old to deal with," Mom adds.

"Yeah, give me a battle with screaming directors, stressed camera operators, edgy horses, unwieldy swords, tired actors and blood gushing everywhere over elementary school any day," Dad says.

I give him a long hard stare.

"Okay, this is a problem mountain, and we need to tackle it one thing at a time," Mom says.

"First," Dad continues. "We all need hot chocolate and cookies!"

A few minutes later, there are three steaming mugs and a plate of oatmeal cookies sitting on the kitchen table. Mom has her notebook in front of her.

"Okay, what shall we tackle?" Mom says.

We decide on the chandelier. Mom writes down 'three hundred dollars.'

"It's not that much any more," I say. "Ivan and I had savings, and I've earned fourteen dollars and seventy-five cents from parkour, and twenty-five cents from lemonade so we're down to fifty nine dollars and seventy-three cents."

"Wow! You're nearly there," Dad says.

"It doesn't feel like it," I mumble. "I should pay more than Ivan. The accident was more my fault than his, and he's paying most of it."

"I think it's great you're helping. Let's make a list of all the things you can do to make money," Mom suggests.

Dad and I smile. Mom has lists for everything, chores, goals, she even has a 'what not to buy' list when she goes shopping. Now we make a 'Chandelier Repayment' list.

Parkour 25c per lesson, siblings 10c

Clean car $5

Shovel snow from driveway $2 (if it snows again)

Wash dishes $1

Ironing 10c each piece of clothing

Dad grabs the notebook from Mom, and adds:

Pluck Dad's nose hairs $10

"This isn't something to laugh about," Mom says. "Maddie, you've got to stop copying your dad."

Dad gives Mom a 'not now' look.

Mom gets up and starts washing the dishes in silence. Her jaw's clenched. She'll get a headache later. I've made her hate Dad, and he's pretending not to notice. *I must make her proud of him again.*

"This's a pretty good list. Where shall we start? Washing Mom's car?" Dad asks.

"Sure," I say.

My brain whirs as we collect a bucket, sponge and soap. *If only Mom could see what I love about Dad. That's it! My hero project for Mr. Phillips! That'll show her how brilliant Dad is. Now all I need is an A for Drama, even Leila's dad thinks As make staying together worthwhile.*

"Dad?" I ask. "How can we make our play brilliant without practicing?"

"Well, proper preparation prevents poor performance," Dad says.

"I know. But we can't rehearse at any of our houses."

"With your problem solving skills, you'll find a way," Dad says.

"I guess."

We'll have to find a secret place. Away from Raquel, Mme Perdu and Mr. Richardson.

"Of course, that's it! I have an idea!"

11

EVACUATE THE BUILDING!

On the day of our show, I'm creeping up the fire exit leading from the basketball court to the gym.

"Ivan, you go first. Leila stay here, as lookout, until we get the door open," I say.

Mme Perdu's facing away from us and looking down at her phone. *She's the best duty aid around.* Ivan squeezes his fingers into the tiny gap in the fire doors. Once open, he picks up the sock I jammed into the doors at the end of PE.

Leila and George run up the stairs and race inside.

"See, I told you I'd get us inside to practice," I say. "Now, let's set up."

I take off my coat, and hand Ivan the two dollars and twenty-five cents from today's parkour lessons. "Just thirteen dollars and forty-eight cents to go."

"That's nothing," Ivan says.

"But your mom's coming to see the show today."

"Leave the rest to me. I can do anything I set my mind on."

I'm not sure whether to be jealous, or sickened by his confidence. Secretly, I'm relieved Ivan's no longer mad with me about the money. I turn my attention to the stage. George has his Lego pieces and a desk lamp set up on a table. Leila is putting Zeus, Aphrodite and Poseidon behind the curtains with the blond Achilles doll. I roll the shopping cart to the wings, take out my electronic skate-board, ride it to the other side of the stage, and set the broad swords ready for battle. I take a sheet off the pile and attach it to two music stands.

"Adjust the table and lamps so the shadows appear on this," I say to George. "Now, let's try the Trojan horse."

I pass Ivan a horse sock puppet attached to our garden rake and pull a brown blanket over my back.

"Now, I hold on to your waist, you pull the blanket over your shoulders, and around the pole," I explain to Ivan. "Then you move to the city gates."

Ivan takes the blanket and starts walking around the gym. I can only see his heels, and the floor below me. I can feel his body pulling away from me as he gets faster and faster, until my feet leave the floor like a bucking bronco, and the blanket falls to one side.

"That's way too fast," I say. "But you get the idea."

Ivan dumps the Trojan horse in front of the Lego table and grabs George's model horse.

"Neigh! Accept me as a gift. An enormous horse statue that's big enough for Greek soldiers to hide in. Hey, if you Trojans are stupid enough to fall for this trick you deserve to lose," Ivan says, grabs a sword, and creates an enormous shadow of a soldier dying from a stab wound.

"What are you children doing in here?"

I swing around to see Mrs. McIntyre, our school administrator, standing at the door. She's glaring over the rim of her glasses.

"We're setting up for our play this afternoon," I reply. "We have a dress rehearsal after recess so we're just getting the stage ready."

"Does Mr. Phillips know you are here?" Mrs. McIntyre asks.

"Sure," Ivan lies, poking his head around the shadow puppet sheet.

"Hmm, Mr. Vladivenski," Mrs. McIntyre says. "I hope he does, for your sake."

"Come on. Let's rehearse the play. We may not have much time," I say. "Shouldn't we get out of here?" Leila panics.

"No. Mrs. McIntyre's old, she'll forget why she came up here before she's at the bottom of the stairs," I reply. "Now, let's start with the gods blessing Achilles."

We spread out the blue material. Ivan and I hold the giant god puppets and stagger towards the river with the baby doll. When I lean the Aphrodite puppet forward, her head lolls, knocks the doll out of my hand, and lands with a thud on my foot. *Ouch! This is meant to make Achilles immortal not brain damaged.*

"You know it was Achilles' mother who dipped him in the water, don't you?" George says.

"Yes! You told us!" I say. "But not until I'd spent a whole weekend finishing three giant god puppets. Now we have the gods, we're going to use them, and no one will know the difference, unless you tell them."

I pick up the doll by the ankle, hold Aphrodite's pole in one hand and thump the doll onto the material. "There, you're immortal. Now let's get on to Helen's story."

I walk across the stage holding the 'twenty years later' sign.

"Leila, come on stage, and brush your hair," I say. "Then George, come up behind her with my dad's dagger, and force her into the chariot."

Leila enters. Her toga looks like a sari, and her long black hair flows over her shoulder. *Wow! She's beautiful! Probably more beautiful than Helen.* George pushes the shopping cart chariot onto the stage behind Leila, draws the dagger out of its silver sheath and forces Leila into captivity.

"Maddie," Leila calls. "I can't get in the cart."

"And I'm Greek," George adds. "Why would I take Helen away from Greece?"

"Leila, just stand on the front bar, and hold on, like little kids do in the grocery store," I say. "And George, you're acting. We've given you the part with the fewest lines, so you can work all the Lego pieces. Ivan's the Greek declaring war on Troy, and George, you're working Greek Lego ships. Let's just try to get through this."

The shadow puppet light switches on, and Ivan makes a great speech about returning Helen or facing the consequences. *He's definitely heard a lot of speeches about 'consequences.' OMG! There's still the issue of the money we owe to Mrs. Vladivenski. She'll be at school this afternoon. I really wanted to pay her back at the show. She'll see how brilliant our play is, get the money, and forgive me. How's Ivan planning to make thirteen dollars and forty-eight cents stuck in here, rehearsing?*

"And so the Greeks went to war," Ivan finishes.

George's Lego soldiers start dancing across the shadow puppet sheets, and Leila shakes a box of knives and forks together to make the sound of clashing weapons.

That's my cue! I grab my broad sword and run on stage. Ivan and I clash high, low, to each side; we spin, jump, move into backbends, and duck under swinging swords.

"Ha! You can't kill me! I'm Achilles, and the gods have protected me!" Ivan shouts.

I lunge forward and drive my sword into the floor just by Ivan's leg. Down he falls, grasping his heel. Achilles is down! I take my broad sword in two hands, Ivan rolls onto his back, and I drive the sword into the space between his ribs and upper arms. Ivan's upper body lifts from the floor, and you can see the tip of the sword sticking out of his back. *If this was a film we could add loads of squirting blood.*

"Now, drag yourself off stage, lie on my electric skateboard, and use it to move across the stage, as if the Trojans are showing Achilles' dead body to the Greeks," I say. "The ribbons are your blood. Make them flow out behind you, but look dead."

Ivan follows my instructions, presses the skateboard switch, and flies at full speed, red ribbons fluttering, from one side of the stage to the other. He's moving so fast he forgets to press the brakes, catches the desk lamp cable between his legs, sends Lego pieces flying, gets tangled in the horse blanket, and crashes, feet first, into the wall.

"Is the skateboard okay?" I ask.

"Look at my Lego!" George squeals.

"Anyone want to know how I am?" Ivan asks.

"We should get out of here," Leila says. "Someone will have heard that."

We stop and listen. No footsteps. No rush of voices. We're safe.

"Let's get set up, and try that again," I say.

Ivan slowly gets to his feet. I take the skateboard and check it's working.

"You only have to press the button lightly," I say. "Just practice on the hall floor while George is setting up. But be careful. This board is irreplaceable."

"It wasn't my fault," Ivan says. "The toga got caught in the controls."

"Whatever," I say.

"Maddie, can you smell burning?" Leila asks.

"Someone probably burnt popcorn in the staff room," I say. "I've heard teachers watch movies all lunchtime, and send us kids into the rain so they're not disturbed."

"But Maddie..." Leila says.

I turn around and see smoke appearing from the wings. *Where there's smoke there's...*

"Fire!" I shout. "Run for it!"

Ivan and Leila bolt for the fire exit, taking off their togas as they leave. George sweeps all his Lego pieces into his Rubbermaid box and runs to join them. I look around, and grab the fire extinguisher hanging on the wall. *If I'm quick, I'll be able to put this out before anyone knows it's happened.*

I can see the problem. The desk lamp must have fallen on the blanket, and the material has started to smolder. I turn the extinguisher upside down in my arms, hold the hose at the smoking horse blanket, and brace myself for the force. *This will be out in no time. Squeeze the trigger gently, and I'll be in control. Time to be a firefighter!*

A piercingly loud fire alarm rings as I bring my fingers and thumb together. I jump and close my fist. The force of the fire extinguisher sends me backwards, tripping over my toga, and landing me on my back, shooting foam high into the air.

"Oh no! Get up! Get this fire out, and get out of here!" I shout at myself, but it's too late.

"Madeleine Moore!" Mr. Richardson's voice booms from the doorway.

Mr. Phillips runs forward, grabs the extinguisher, and points it at the smoldering blanket. Foam covers the smoke. The fire is out, but for me the danger has just begun. I stand slowly and face the principal. My eyes sting from the smoke and humiliation. I can hear sirens approaching the school.

"We need to evacuate the building," Mr. Richardson says. "Round up the kids and check attendance."

I turn to leave.

"You, Madeleine Moore, can stay right by my side," Mr. Richardson orders. "You have some explaining to do to the fire chief, and me."

12

THE SHOW MUST GO ON

I found out eighty-eight and a half minutes ago I was allowed to perform in the show. Since then it's been talk, talk, talk. First, I had a meeting with Mr. Richardson and the fire chief, then it was me and my principal, and I've just met with Mr. Richardson, Mom and Dad. I've missed the dress rehearsal. *Why do grown-ups take so long to sort out an accident? An accident where no one got hurt!*

I look up at Mom. She's not smiling. I bet there'll be more words at home. She'll probably blame Dad unless I can show her how great he is.

The walk from the office to the hall is long and slow. With each step I think about all the unsolved problems — *Mom and Dad are obviously unhappy. They'll split up, and it'll be my fault. We don't have three hundred dollars for Mrs. Vladivenski, so Ivan'll still have a 'no friends to play' rule — my fault. Raquel's play will be better than ours and Leila won't get an A because I wasn't there to rehearse — my fault again!*

I was relieved when Mr. Phillips talked Mr. Richardson out of suspension. Now that I have to enter the gym, two days at home seems like a great idea.

"I'd usually say 'break a leg,' but I think 'good luck' is more appropriate today," Dad says.

"Yes, good luck," Mom says.

I enter the gym, closely followed by Mr. Richardson, Mom and Dad. Ivan cheers, and everyone looks in my direction. I feel my face redden. Leila and George are grinning.

"Thank you for coming this afternoon," Mr. Phillips says. "I apologize for the unexpected delay. But now we're all here, please sit back, and enjoy the work grade five have done on heroes."

I slide into the seat next to Leila, Mr. Phillips moves to his laptop, and the lights are turned off. The song that Raquel recorded with Dom the Dude plays through the loudspeaker. My enemy is bouncing up and down in her seat exchanging thumbs-up signs with our drama teacher. We catch each others' eye, and she gives me an evil look. *What have I done now?*

Images of our projects appear on the screen. Leila's work on Gandhi is first, followed by images of work done on the hockey player, Wayne Gretsky, and the Lego founder, Ole Kirk Christiansen.

"Okay, pay up," Ivan whispers to Yan Yan.

Something is being passed along from kid to kid. *Is it a note? I don't think so.* I can see something moving from one fist into another. *What is it?* Then, one by one, loonies are being placed in the Rubbermaid box under Ivan's chair. *Money!*

"What's going on?" I ask.

"Ivan took bets on whether you would be suspended," Leila says.

Great. The loonies keep coming. I can see there were a lot of people who believed I wouldn't be here for the show.

"All together, we've got three hundred now," Ivan says. "I told you I'd find a way."

"SHHH!" Raquel says.

"What's up with her?" I ask.

"I made a double or quits bet with her," Ivan says. "If you were suspended, you would've been her slave for two months, and owe her twenty dollars."

"What!" I mouth.

"I knew you'd be here." Ivan smiles. "So you're off the hook."

"Thanks. I think."

Mr. Phillips catches my eye and points to the screen. I turn around. It's my iMovie. The words 'My Hero' spin around then come into focus as my voice-over starts.

My hero isn't famous, like Anjolie or Brad,

My superman and champion, said simply is my dad.

A rotating photo of Dad takes over the title on the

screen. I slide down in my seat. Blood rushes to my face, but movies don't give any recovery time. *This is such a bad idea. Mom'll hate Dad even more after this.*

He can pull a wheelie, be a knight…

Clips of Dad's wheelie in *Cinderella,* and a broadsword fight from *A Knight of the Realm* play out in front of me. Whoops and cheers come from my class. I want to disappear into a sinkhole.

"Your dad is SO cool," Ivan says.

A smile creeps across my face. I sit up so I can see the next sequence where I'm practicing wheelies on my BMX. I know what's coming next.

But I'll work with all my might,

I'll draw my swords and parry

'Til skills are legendary.

There I am, at All Action Inc with a wooden broadsword, moving slowly through the practice moves.

"Go, Maddie," shouts Stu from the front seat.

Others copy him, and I'm surrounded with "Way to go, Maddie!" and "Awesome!" Some nervous laughter comes from the moms and dads sitting behind us.

My dad can set the world on fire

It's him that I admire…

"Wow!" comes a chorus of shouts from the audience as Dad leaps from a burning building, his clothing covered in flames.

"Oh, no!" comes from the adults, and my friends gasp as they watch me jump from the patio, dressed as Hero, with my costume burning. *I really am becoming like my dad.*

I glance over my shoulder. Mom's wiping a tear from her face. She leans over and whispers something in Dad's ear.

But the best thing in the world must be,

He completes our family tree.

Dad puts his arm around Mom, and she moves closer to him. There on the screen is a photo of Mom, Dad and me in front of our Christmas tree.

It worked!

The lights come on, and Mr. Phillips moves the screen away from the stage. Raquel sneers at me.

"What?" I mouth at her.

"Ignore her," Leila whispers. "We're going first."

I look up at the stage. There's the blue material for our river, and the white shadow puppet sheet with a corner burnt out of it. *It's time for the show.*

"This term, we've been very lucky. Dominic Drummond from 3D Acting for Life came to teach us some drama. Some of the rehearsals have been a little bit more dramatic than we wanted," Mr. Phillips says. "But I'm sure you'll agree the children have worked hard, learned a lot, and gained valuable experience. Thank you, Dominic."

Dominic stands, and takes a bow. Raquel waves at her drama teacher, who's blowing kisses to our class. *Ergh! Moms and dads should be the only people who blow kisses at kids. And they should stop by grade three.*

"Now, we'll start our Stories from Around the World with the Greek legend, The Trojan Wars," Mr. Phillips continues.

We shuffle out of our seats. Leila, George and Ivan are already in their togas, so they help me into my sheet. We pick up Zeus, Aphrodite and Poseidon. The play is underway.

George kidnaps Leila, and the shopping cart chariot gets safely across the stage. Ivan declares war, and the Lego shadow puppets show the Greeks heading to Troy. The Lego battle moves smoothly into Achilles' downfall. My heart's beating loudly, and my lines come out of my mouth so quickly I can't breathe.

"Remember to speak slowly, clearly, and loudly." Mom's breakfast advice comes back to me.

The sounds coming from the audience fill me with excitement. I can hear cheers, gasps, and nervous giggles as Achilles is paraded very slowly in front of the Greek army, on the electric skateboard with red ribbons trailing behind him.

I peek out from the wings. I can see Mom and Dad laughing, crying and looking at each other. They look so happy. I think of when they met, acting together at school. Dad leans over and kisses Mom. *Yes! My mom and dad are in love! I did it!*

"Come on," Ivan says. "We have to be the horse."

When Ivan and I step on stage with our horse's head, and singed blanket, an enormous cheer goes up from the audience. George comes on stage and takes the present of the Trojan horse into the wings. Then shows the Lego gift heading through the Trojan city wall.

"Take that!" I shout from off stage, then run on stage and pretend to kill Trojans in their beds.

I'm leaping around the stage, stabbing, hacking and slashing, while Leila, Ivan and George are pretending to die in the wings. Their groans and moans are just about covering the sound of their giggling. Then I grab Leila by the hand and drag her on stage.

"It's time to take you home," I declare.

The audience breaks into cheers. George and Ivan join us on stage, and we take our bow.

Oh, this feels good! I look out into the gym. Boys in my class are copying the death noises, Mom and Dad are on their feet clapping. Mr. Phillips and Mr. Richardson are looking at each other, and smiling as they clap. Everyone looks happy. Well, everyone except Raquel, who is sitting, crossing her arms, and holding an enormous mermaid's tail close to her chest.

The rest of the performance is a bit of a blur. I'm in my seat watching it, but a bubble has formed around me. *I did it!* There's a warm, gooey feeling inside me as I replay the best moments in my mind. It's as if all other sounds are on mute, and the acting is in slow motion. I wake up briefly when Morgan falls off his throne. But mostly, there's just me, and the feeling of victory.

Finally, Raquel comes on stage for the last scene in their play. A recorded voice-over plays, "Legs, no voice, I left my life for a dream, and have ended with nothing. No love, no family, no place to call home." Is this the version Sunshine and Raine were told as kids? It definitely isn't Disney.

The audience is silent. Everyone is listening to Raquel's recorded words. They're so sad, and she's completely still on stage. I hate to admit it, but she's good, very good.

I clap with everyone else.

"As you can see, grade five has worked hard. Thank you to all the parents who have opened their homes for rehearsals, and lent a hand with costumes and props," Mr.

Phillips says. "But we have one special thank you. Raquel, would you like to come up here?"

Raquel stands.

"I'd like to thank Dominic for coming to our school, and teaching drama to us," Raquel announces. "This show would not have been possible without you. On the count of three, everyone. One, two, three..."

My whole class jump to their feet and shout, "Thank you, Dom the Dude!"

I am a second behind. They must've practiced this when I was with the principal.

"Thank you, thank you," Dominic says. "There's some real talent in this class, and it's been my pleasure to work with you all. But now my creative juices need to be poured into writing. If any of you want to join my drama school, we're going to win the next Young Filmmaker of the Year Award with its amazing theme, *It was a dark and stormy night...*"

There's polite laughter, and applause from the grown-ups. Chairs start scraping on the gym floor. Parents and children move towards each other, and the hum of congratulations grow.

I half run and half skip to Mom and Dad, and throw my arms around them.

"Maddie, we're so proud of you," Dad says. "And I'm touched you chose me as your hero."

"Touched," Mom echoes with tears in her eyes.

"That was quite a show," Dad continues.

"And you stuck at it through thick and thin," Mom says, finding her voice again.

"Oh, that reminds me," I say.

I run back to Ivan's chair, pick up the Rubbermaid box, and weave my way through the crowd. I grab Leila's hand and catch George's eye.

"Come on," I say.

Ivan's mom is standing near the exit, looking tall and formal in her smart business suit. She must have come straight from her office.

I stand in front of her, scraping my feet on the floor. Then realize Mom and Dad are right there with me. Smiling. Their presence makes me feel a little braver. I take a deep breath.

"Madeleine, vot a show!" Mrs. Vladivenski smiles.

"Thanks."

I have to get this over with. My heart's racing. I hold the box out towards Ivan's mom. It feels heavy with three hundred dollars in quarters, loonies and a few five-dollar notes.

"This is for you. I'm really, really, really sorry about the chandelier. We'll be more careful, and clear more space next time."

"Next time?" Mrs. Vladivenski asks. "You're planning a next time?"

"Of course! We have to win the Young Filmmaker of the Year Award. And I have an idea!"

ABOUT THE AUTHOR

Sonia Garrett lives in Vancouver, Canada with her stuntman husband and their daughter. She has worked as a dancer, clown, actor, drama teacher and franchise owner for Gymboree Play and Music. Now, Sonia seems to have settled down to being a mom, Montessori teacher, storyteller and writer.

Sonia loves visiting schools, speaking to writers and building relationships with readers.

If you enjoyed *Maddie Makes Money* please post a short review on Amazon.com

Books by Sonia Garrett:
Maddie Makes a Movie
Maddie Makes Money

To connect with Sonia please visit:
www.soniagarrett.ca
sonia@soniagarrett.ca